To Dad

[handwritten signature]

Batu Breye 2010

M000038923

Copyright © 2007 by Piero Rivolta
All rights reserved

Printed in the United States of America
by New Chapter Publisher
Rivolta, Piero
Sunset in Sarasota/Piero Rivolta
ISBN (13-digit) 978-0-9792012-0-2
ISBN (10-digit) 0-9792012-0-9

Sunset in Sarasota available for sale at:

www.amazon.com

Also by Piero Rivolta:

Just One Scent: The Rest is God

Alex and the Color of the Wind (in Italian; available
in English in late 2007)

For more information about Piero Rivolta, visit:
www.pierorivolta.net

It is very important for me to acknowledge all the people who have been so patient to put up with me in the process of transforming a manuscript into a real book and marketing it. Unfortunately, the only way I know how to interpret my thoughts is to put them down on paper with fountain pen; I am very meticulous in what I write, but my handwriting is horrible. I hope Bill Gates will forgive me.

A special thank-you goes to John Rugman, an American who has chosen to live in Turin, Italy; Cristina Visconti who has the office next to mine and helps me all the time; Su Byron and Kim Northrop, who were able to get this book to the printer; and, last, but not least, my dear long-time friend Richard Storm, who continues to take care of my public relations, even though he is semi-retired.

A super important acknowledgment goes to my wife, Rachele, who, with all her fiery and unpredictable character, over more than 40 years, has continued to spark in me all kinds of reactions, doubts, sentiments and questions. Perhaps I am a masochist but I still love her a lot.

Piero Rivolta
Winter, 2006

To Sarasota that I love so much.

SUNSET

IN

SARASOTA

PIERO RIVOLTA

C H A P T E R 1

That day Albert turned 50.

It was a Saturday. He was sitting at his usual table in a corner of the living room, in front of a window.

From his tenth-floor apartment he could see buildings of every size and semblance. Beyond some towered large trees; green swaths stretched out, with tiny squares and straight roads that intersected at right angles. Cutting across the cheerful disarray, typical of the cities of Florida in continuous flux and change, the line of the sea could be seen darting between one edifice and the next. His building was smack in the middle of all of the life of the city, four blocks from the bay, which was dotted with several islands. The long ones to the west formed a barrier that separated the waters of the bay proper from the turquoise waters of the Gulf of Mexico.

Judging from the height of the sun, it must have been about two or three in the afternoon. It being early February, the weather was pleasant and mild. The breeze that blew through the open windows caressed everything it touched, and even seemed to bring to life the leaves of a silk plant that had been placed beside the open glass door leading to Albert's balcony. He'd been living in that condo for two years. It never ceased to amaze him how everything in this city was wrapped in a penetrating light, at times direct and blaring, and at others shadowy and dif-fused—but always penetrating.

The sun began its descent into the sea towards the west, the direction in which Albert's living room windows faced. It was the typical massive, alive, stubbornly round sun of Florida's west coast.

Who knows why only in this place it seemed so round to him, homogeneous and blaring, while at the same time malleable, as if during its journey the sun had to adapt itself somewhat to the atmosphere. Later, a strange yellowy color would spread across the sky—and over the city—for which he failed to find an explanation. He had seen lots of suns and sunsets in lots of cities, but only here had he noticed that peculiar yellow.

This was probably due to the fact that Sarasota lay at about the same latitude as Egypt, where, for thousands of years, an intense yellow light had inspired a people moved by grand instincts to worship the blazing Sun God.

~~~

As his eyes and spirit filled with such sensations, he suddenly felt very sad and waxed pensive. His soul fed and thrived on a form of mysterious premonition. He always saw the beautiful side of this world. He believed what people said, also because he was easily able to read into their souls and discard, without realizing it, that which he perceived as false or deviated. The negative side of others' personalities passed by Albert without so much as grazing him.

After so many years work in high finance, after so much hustling, a whole new world was opening up to him. Suddenly it had become extremely difficult for him to understand why many people created so many problems and took pleasure in fighting just to feel alive, indispensable and thus important.

He realized only then how often he had failed to notice that the sun was in the sky and that it moved, and how large and powerful it was, and that it was there not merely to alternately mark night and day. After all, not noticing that doesn't make it any less important!

Of course, this doesn't mean that the sun is always a completely positive force, either. Surely it is necessary, but we certainly do not know that it is always positive. For instance, what about when its heat unleashes a hurricane or dries up the land? How can those events ever be positive?

Here opens a debate as long as the very existence of humanity itself. We might say that the hurricanes generated by the sun's heat are necessary, because they pilfer humidity from the sea and send it raining down on lands in need of it. But couldn't some other system, less violent and wrathful, have been found? Where's the logic to it? What happens to our subconscious search for simplicity in life, that search in which there is an answer to every question?

Reasoning thus, what we do find is a way to justify humanity, which creates new mechanisms to complicate individuals' lives every day.

Sometimes there arise temporary cycles of atonement—talk of love and understanding—but then the system plows on, and that same talk is used to create new traps and complications for the chump who still thinks he's living in the previous cycle, the so-called love cycle.

Albert looked out his window and experienced a vision of sorts, which seemed to concretize his thoughts. The colors grew lusterless, the light became cloudy. The cycle of love faded in the sun. He sat immobile, as if turned to stone, incredulous that he had been able to grasp such a well-defined and visual phenomenon, which reflected what for days had been happening within him—love was fading in the sun.

Indeed, he was so grim, so uptight that he had not

noticed the mass of clouds thickening over the city.

Doggedly, he repeated out loud, "It's true, love fades in the sun."

~~~

Two years before, he had moved to that sweet little city on the west coast of Florida called Sarasota. It was as if he had been immersed in an unreal world.

Living there was belonging to the life of an island from which all the world's activity could be seen, and participating only in those activities you were interested in, only the ones you liked. The undesirable activities just brush by you, as if you were watching them on TV.

At the same time, people came to this "island" bringing with them interesting, highly qualified backgrounds. Nearly all of the new arrivals were fired up with the enthusiasm and the drive to consider themselves competitors in the creation of a lifestyle and its ensuing occurrences that usually was only ever seen in big sophisticated cities. The strange thing was, they actually succeeded.

The longer you lived there, the more you realized it wasn't an island at all, but a part of terra firma, which comprised the American as well as the European continent—albeit ideally—in that the Europeans, being newcomers, had only been partially Americanized.

An island is like the bottom of a valley where a

road comes to an end. Though it may be connected to the rest of the world via computers, telephones, airplanes and ships, it never seems to be able to shake off its "island complex." This is the air you breathe there—you sense it in the words of its people—it comes through in every climatic event.

In Sarasota, the large, flat, wooded stretch of Florida was present and palpable, as if it bore down on the shoulders of the city. It was only a matter of driving east a few miles past the highway and everything became endless green country. It did end, however, when you hit Florida's east coast. But till then, you could drive for miles over the flatlands in the middle of nothingness without seeing a soul, except for an isolated town here or there, where, passing through, you might ask yourself how the devil it ever wound up so shiftless yet still remained.

Not that Sarasota didn't have its problems, too. People suffered there, some barely survived; people died there, people killed, and killed themselves. It had its good, its less good, and its bad, like everywhere else in the world—without them, of course, humanity, even life itself, would never exist. Everybody's playing the same game, and many times the roles are not clear; they are exchanged, confused.

But as strange as it may seem, in Sarasota people seemed to play that game in a different tone.

People were courteous, though at times falsely so; what counted, at any rate, was the result, the thing you can touch and perceive. Many people apparently wanted to make their contribution to the community—a high percentage, judging by the frequency of events held and the number of participants. Indeed, it may have given one the impression that behind all this was a community with the size and financial power of Atlanta or even New York. This was the impression that Sarasota often gave to people from larger cities who came to town to participate in some of the local events.

For Sarasota and its inhabitants it seemed natural. They may not even have noticed it anymore, so widespread was this phenomenon among the different groups and social strata. This may have been the result of wanting to live as intensely as possible until the last instant of one's life, or perhaps it was the desire to show off, or some latent, looming sense of pride. Whatever its cause, the phenomenon was real. And even if personal pettiness concealed itself behind that facade, the end result was positive.

That is what counts, always—as long as the evolution of life can never be taken seriously. Life? It's too silly, inexplicable and fickle. At a certain point you draw your conclusion, but we'll never know whether it's real or fake. One day our deck of cards will be reshuffled and then maybe we'll understand. For now, all we've got to do is live.

~~~

In Sarasota, people go around saying, "Another day in paradise!"—even if in this paradise people suffer and die like everywhere else. In truth, it's not like everywhere else. This all seems almost fake, as if you really were living in paradise and your next destination might be Earth.

Albert figured it was a legacy bequeathed to the city by John Ringling himself, the man who, in the 1920's, had put this city on the map of the United States. Upon his death, he left an important museum behind, an eccentric home, and a wealth of interesting things. Most of all, though, he had given this city its soul. His number-one passion had been the circus. And it's certainly no gamble to imagine that it was the circus that impregnated the life of this locality with illusions, creating a system that seemed only to just graze reality. Perhaps people still felt like jugglers, magicians or clowns destined to mask over their own sadness and to allow only a joyous spirit shine through.

When it came down to it, it didn't matter much at all. After spending a lifetime in a world where a sense of humor is considered a depravation, Albert accepted this new sensation with joy, even if its true origins continued to remain a mystery.

CHAPTER 2

Albert was born in Rhode Island to a well-to-do family. His father had founded a law office which, over the years, had become highly regarded in the area. He had attended local schools, where the work came easy to him; and it was an easy life for him at the home of his paternal ancestors, where he had many friends. He'd also made friends with the children of vacationers who came to Newport, as well with as the children of some of his father's business contacts. Most came from the northeastern states. These friends would have a remarkable influence on his future.

He was accepted at Harvard and enrolled. He went on to law school, where he specialized in international business law. He didn't know why, but inside him he felt a push toward the concept of the "globality" of the world. He also thought that the most common language, and the most homogeneous concepts were those that had to do with business and economics. Sure, there were lots of political parties, many governments, loads of ideas, a host of divinities, but there was only one terrestrial God that made the world go round: money.

It didn't matter if it was real or just on paper; or whether transactions were concrete or just convoluted; or whether money brought a positive result and provided something useful for humanity; or whether it remained like castles in the air to the advantage of a few wise guys. In reality, this particular language was more or less spoken throughout the world. Some people spoke in trillions of dollars—whose value was pretty much impossible to conceive. Others spoke in billions or perhaps millions, while many—most—were absorbed with much smaller amounts. Of course, it was better to be up in the trillions or billions. That world was so abstract that it made it difficult to isolate the errors and distortions of the system. Everything could be reorganized so that it looked all right, even if such a project revealed holes not forecast by the budget.

Most importantly, in these dizzying financial realms, the companies and nations involved were forced to collaborate in order to avoid a catastrophe of unimaginable proportions.

The lower the monetary value, the more concrete problems there were about making payment deadlines and respecting time limits, which become real and pressing. In these lower realms there was hardly any chance of pulling off the most acrobatic solutions. Worst of all, the numbers on paper took on the descriptions of real people, actual human faces in real situations. Such manifestations would haunt your dreams and jeopardize your family's serenity.

Albert certainly did not want that. He would remain in what was referred to as "high finance," which, when it comes down to it, is pretty much the only activity that is shared throughout the globe, normally so fragmented and litigious in all the rest. Perhaps scientific research might also be considered an international language, but in the end this activity is also regulated by high finance marketing.

At last, a single common religion had been found, for which men argue and fight—virtually, that is. Whether one faction wins and another faction loses, the equilibrium more or less remains the same, of interest to all.

The only things that change are the names of groups and nations that count more than the others, but basically the whole system remains constant and beyond the comprehension of individuals. The system may be compared to a ship sailing round the ocean, making slight variations in its course, stopping now at one port, then at another to refuel.

In those days, Albert was too focused on trying to guarantee himself a lifetime of security to imagine that there might exist other international languages—art, music, love, and so on.

These are tough themes to tackle; in fact, they are themes that have been used to pit mankind against itself on many occasions. Think, for example, of the Scottish bagpipes playing at the onset of a battle and to celebrate victories in war; or those artists with huge marketing efforts behind them; or the studied message of love used by well-organized religions in order to wield power.

~~~

His upbringing had been overly pragmatic, his world vision limited to the situations of the area where he lived, where people thought much of themselves indeed, and believed that the competition was confined to a restricted group of persons who—imagine that!—all happened to be located along the east coast, north of New York City.

The rules of business, as well, were applied differently to those who did not happen to have the good fortune of being born there, or at least to reside in that place for a good number of years and be accepted as one of their own.

But there was something different about Albert.

He looked out at the world.

After coming home from college he realized for the first time that to reach his home from anywhere else in the world, he had to cross a bridge. He had grown up among bridges, yet it had never dawned on him that the state of Rhode Island really was an island, just as its name so clearly indicated. Suddenly he began to quake. He did not want to be an islander with an islander's mentality.

Through some old friends he found a job in New York, in one of those large companies that have interests everywhere in practically everything. A young single man with a Harvard education, who longed to see the world and was ready to hop the next flight, even in the middle of the night, to go anywhere his job took him to defend the interests of the organization he belonged to certainly made him a fine acquisition.

He worked that job for exactly 20 years. Indeed, 20 years and one day after he was hired, he suddenly realized, thanks to a series of occurrences that make up this story, that there also existed something called "sense of humor." He began to laugh. He laughed at what his life had been up till then, at the things he had been taught and at his tasks and responsibilities. So as not to be suffocated by laughter, he quit his job.

He immediately stopped laughing.

For the very first time in his life he found himself alone, without the support of the system, without the tags of vice president or president or CEO attached to his name to confirm his importance. He suddenly discovered he was still a young man, especially when he removed his dark suits and let his hair grow a little.

He was 45. His parents had died not long before, one after the other. They had brought him into the world when they weren't so young anymore. His father had been the first to go, at 86. His mother, perhaps tired of living by herself in that big house in Rhode Island, had followed him, at the age of 80. He had no brothers or sisters.

At 45 he was alone. He didn't have to wear dark suits anymore and he was financially well off. He had earned lots of money during those 20 years of hard work. He also had access to a considerable family trust fund left to him by his father, and had learned plenty of tricks of the trade on how invest his own money. That day, the word "tricks" seemed especially appropriate, because they referred to capital written across a computer screen, money floating among the airwaves, sensitive to all sorts of news and events, no matter how extraneous to the true value of a given share of a given company or financial organization. But that was fine. People fell for it, he knew his way around and had reached a level of independence that he never could have dreamed of.

~~~

The only real problem was that for the first time he began to think intensely and stopped laughing altogether.

He threw himself into reading—books that had nothing to do with his former job. He had discovered a new pleasure. He read whatever he could find.

Enough business reports, contracts, books on economics and politics, and worst of all, newspapers! He simply read whatever else he came across, and listened to a little music. Just a little, though, since getting accustomed to music took time. It was necessary to feel music, until it became an addiction. But it was hard to understand; sometimes it grew boring. He still had to find his kind of music.

One day, while reading Herman Hesse's Steppenwolf, he was struck by a concept the author takes up from Novalis, which went something like this: Men are born to live on the earth. By nature, they have no desire to think. Indeed, they are born to live, not to think. Those who think, who break life down in terms of pure thought may go far, it is true, but they take water for land and are doomed to drown.

Albert had seen a good part of the world—but not the way a tourist sees it.

He had lived it. He had dealt with the local people, learned to communicate with them, strained to understand what they wanted or what they thought in order to sell them the right product or use them to produce something in accordance with their capacities which could be sold somewhere else.

Nothing easy in all that. You had to listen, observe, experiment. Why, in a certain sense it was an almost psychological job.

In reality, that's what he was, a particular kind of psychologist who had at his disposal the power of the financial organization that was behind him. And while he did have to listen, he could also use the power of money, advertising and public relations to impose. The financial means were never lacking. One way or another, if it was worth it, they could be procured on the world market.

Now, no matter how well-off he may have been, he was by himself. He would have to reckon with others, but mostly with himself.

He came to the conclusion that he was truly alone and did not have a clear focus on what values were to provide him with joy and sadness, with gratification and defeat—those experiences that make us feel alive.

Giving up such a promising career had required much determination. It seemed that climbing the steps of the world of high finance had become very natural for him. Why had all his resolute desire suddenly vanished? It may have been that since he had no family to have to care about, he was left with more room to think and dwell on the type of existence he'd led. Surely Hermann Hesse was right-thinking leads to drowning. Thinking leads you to see how ridiculous the world is, even in its most profound misfortunes.

Now he sat before his living room window, book in hand, watching the sun on its way toward its daily plunge into the waters of the Gulf of Mexico.

CHAPTER 3

Even when one suddenly awakens and makes that decision to get out of his or her life's routine, it takes time to get a grip on what it is one really wants. People grope through travels, revisiting stereotypes linked to their pasts.

From the cold of cities like Chicago and New York, which had once been the bases from which he would set out for South and Central America, Asia, the Middle East, Europe and Australia, he decided to take the route that many others had taken—move to Florida.

After a certain period of indecision, he had chosen Sarasota.

He had already been there more than once. Unlike Florida's east coast beaches, Sarasota's ultra-white beaches had awed him. They were clean and serene, and the color of the Gulf of Mexico reminded him somewhat of the Mediterranean, of which he had fond memories.

He'd also marveled at the city's pleasant, fairly relaxed atmosphere, and was especially delighted with the city's interest in the arts. He decided to explore this new horizon more thoroughly. Up till then, his familiarity extended only as far as a glimpse of the mundane side. Indeed, wherever he went he'd always try to seek out the local arts scenes, only as a spectator, and with discreet curiosity.

Of course, intelligence begets curiosity.

In Sarasota his aim now was to observe this world from within. It would surely be easier to get on the inside track in a small city like Sarasota than in an all too well-oiled and complex machine such as New York. This was a world somewhat different from the world of his snob friends, who experienced art and theater only as mundane events, or as simple and ephemeral entertainment there to amuse without being overly thought-provoking.

He had seen how many of his older colleagues retired at an advanced age, bought huge houses in some seaside Florida country club; they'd keep another home up north for the summer. Their lives revolved around the country club and their country club friends.

Being alone, and still young, he bought an apartment in a downtown condo near the bay. It wasn't a new building, but it was built well. It offered a good view; its size met his needs. There were two bedrooms, a den, a living room/dining room and kitchen. The whole area around was undergoing rapid growth. In the future he would find something more impressive, though he did not yet know where.

Of course, there were some old friends of his who were also retired, who showed him around. They lived in large homes there about eight months a year. They came from the same world as he did. He spent a lot of time with one in particular, a very lively chap bent on enjoying life. He was married to a much younger woman, had a lovely home in one of the area's most exclusive country clubs, with two golf courses. Albert began frequenting the club, as well. At last, his friend convinced him to become a member, even if it wasn't easy for non-residents to get accepted, the available openings being limited.

But his old friends came through with a miracle. One of them was on the board of directors.

Albert began spending more and more time at the club. He played golf, but played more tennis, which gratified his muscles, put his reflexes to the test. After a couple sets of tennis, tired and sweaty, he felt free of something. He often took lunch at the club, sometimes his friends asked him to join them.

He soon belonged to the club's elite, even if through the side door. Because he was not a resident, he didn't have the right to vote. He was, however, kept abreast of the internal gossip and witnessed violent battles of opinion on how to organize tee time, furnish the club and which occasions to celebrate. Albert learned to never underestimate clashes between the female and male groups. He also learned to respect the internal tensions that plagued the various committees, including those who chose the flower arrangements for parties; those who picked out the cutlery and dishes; those who decided whether to replace a dead tree; and those who scheduled use of the cricket field.

His friends talked constantly of the club. They held meetings in their own homes in the evenings, brainstorming new ways to control the club and its policies.

He heard the comments about various subordinates and the manager, whom he began to consider a masochist who had no doubt chosen that position for himself in order to atone for crimes committed in past lives. In a short time he made the acquaintance of all those who worked at the club and the comments of some members seemed for the most part exaggerated. These employees tried to do a good job, despite the fact that Florida, with its climate, tends to inspire relaxation rather than efficiency.

Generally speaking, it seemed to Albert that everything worked quite well, and apparently with relative ease, despite all the internal tensions. Perhaps it was the cordial and amicable staff that brought a sense of harmony to the club. Albert was impressed with these capable employees who seemed to really want to make others happy.

Today, that's one quality that's hard to come by!

He was well aware of this after having lived in so many different realities, even if he was covered by the umbrella of the firm.

Surely, in his previous position, so cut off from everyday problems and far from actual production, he had passed ruthless judgment upon structures that did not produce enough in economic terms, and indirectly put the screws to the entire hierarchy, from the president to management to every last worker. The whole thing depended only upon a series of numbers, which reached him in graph and table form through the computer. He had only dealt directly with other high finance CEOs, their battles, or better yet, with their tricks—open to any type of compromise that might improve their positions.

Relationships at the country club were different. You rubbed elbows every day with the staff who were there to please you—their job in exchange for a salary. There they were every day. When you smiled at them, they smiled back. If the atmosphere was good, you felt happy.

The same went for the other members, whether they belonged to the A, B or C category, or were simply guests that belonged to no category at all—to be considered transparent, even if the club counted on them for their financial support.

The tough thing to explain was why in a country club of this sort, which should have been a place where people with similar tastes could meet, there should exist such divisions. Some divisions were actually official as they depended on the kind of membership each member possessed. Full members were allowed to participate in all club activities. Then there were tennis-only memberships, and memberships that gave access only to the dining room, the bar and restrooms. These different categories had been devised by the developer to suit a variety of needs and tastes. Those who didn't like golf could sign up for tennis, instead—it cost less, too.

For the man inside the car was driving a Lexus any different than driving a Chevrolet? Can one's difference in social status be determined by a few thousand dollars?

For a long time even Albert had thought this way, but then he realized that many people really didn't care what kind of car they drove. Maybe they were into boats or horses. Either that, or they had no money to spend at all—even if they were brilliant, they just didn't care about what they drove. Such examples may be exaggerations, though in substance they correspond with reality.

Other, non-written categories also existed, which depended on members' seniority, or on whether they had served on the board, or because they were part of a group held in particular consideration, which seemed to be constantly scheming away in order to procure its own advantages. The members of one such group, which Albert found out was called the "High Hats" truly believed they were set apart from the rest.

He realized he'd gotten himself bogged down in a place where you spent your day following the same rules that one followed inside a high finance firm, though could not figure out why. What was there to be gained? What concrete award or personal satisfaction could each of these club members expect?

He came to the conclusion that he was living a farce in which many people enjoyed playing the fool without realizing it.

He had the proof of what he always thought— that cliques formed in the club, and life there became similar to the life they had always known. Members fought among themselves to get elected to the board, to become president or chairman. They used all the tricks they had learned in a lifetime to impose their opinions, create castes, sell their ideas to other members, and so on.

Albert was not able to understand why they wasted so much energy on a club that had been created for the purpose of enjoying life, playing golf and tennis, eating and drinking.

Surely these people missed the structures within the firms they had once worked for, which had fed their needs and satisfied their egos.

By themselves they were nothing.

Now all those people had to sustain their vain ambitions was a ridiculous country club. Albert had already given that lifestyle up on his own.

How could he have taken part in that country club farce?

Luckily, most people weren't like that. For them life at the club was a distraction until it was time to return to work, or their domestic tranquility, or the partial boredom of their lives. Albert, to his discredit, was friends with that tiny minority that did everything in their power to make the club an unreal place. One day he got wind of letters sent to the board of directors, some of which were anonymous, with outlandish declarations and accusations. A friend showed him a sampling. It was the last straw. Albert decided to back off, and with much tact and kindness, abandoned that world. He'd come to realize that there was no place for him there.

~~~

Returning home, downtown was like changing planets. It dawned on him that he'd hardly ever run into any of his club friends at various local theaters. They attended the club's "cultural" events, which, though well organized, remained somewhat homespun and could not compete with the offerings of the city, featuring respected professional artists.

He began making himself scarce around the country club. He did not renew his membership, using the excuse that he wanted to travel. His life now entailed staying at home, walks on the beach, reading, and seeking out curiosities, watering holes, tiny out-of-the-way restaurants, and all sorts of events. He wanted to see people and what they did, get to know them—not as numbers, but as people.

He also wanted to take time out for himself, time out to think.

He forgot that thinking too much could lead to drowning.

His first major doubt concerned his own existence.

Am I a person, a single, unique entity—someone who knows what he wants to do?

Does everybody feel this way?

Or is each of us a compilation of different personalities that sometimes think and act as one, and at other times are in contrast?

Good question.

He began to see the people he frequented in an all-new light. They may not have possessed egos as big as they sought to make the world believe, and perhaps they were actually a bundle of smaller egos more or less tied together.

He would have to reason this out. He would need proof. Through experience with others, Albert would go on to discover himself.

He was at a loss as to how to begin, and what method to use. He sought the answers in his reading, though that same reading sometimes led to greater confusion.

~~~

Christianity claims that we are all children of God, though this may be merely a metaphor to explain something more profound. It may thus be understood that we are a part of God, as a child inherits flesh and blood from his or her parents, as well as—to a certain degree—virtues and defects, bodily health and frailty.

So what is God, then—mother or father? Perhaps both. Or neither of the two, because we are simply part of God. A spark that is cast off and returns to the original mass of light.

If this is true, then God has more than one ego.

If we are sparks flying off from the Everything, then we, too, as tiny as we may be, have also been created in the same way. Unfortunately, we happen to be so very small and insignificant that we have a hard enough time finding all these egos, lost and insecure. At which point we create an ego and work our whole lives to make it solid and big, bigger than ourselves.

If we do not happen to catch on, then all goes well and we continue our lives, happy or sad as they may be, but in any case, with conviction.

But what happens when we ask the first question regarding this topic? Albert did not know for sure. He gave a shudder and closed the balcony door. Not that cold air had been coming through, but outside it looked to Albert as though it were snowing. It was just the gray of the sky that precedes darkness, which advanced from building to building, penetrating the souls of those who are keen observers.

CHAPTER 4

Many a time does man seek out complete independence in his private life, yet he so often finds his spirit enveloped in a sort of solitude that, while it has its pleasant sides, may also harbor moments of profound boredom, which may even lead to states of dismay. Once this point has been reached, a helter-skelter search for another may ensue, one with whom to share such moments, someone whose task it would be to brighten up your life.

But here, the two of you—and that other surely exists—have got a common problem; that is, you both have the same needs.

This someone may be just a friend, male or female, or even a dog or a cat. Actually, a dog is the first step. The beginning of a descent that leads to more complicated relationships, ties that might blossom into something deep, or only something apparently deep, inasmuch as it is sealed and sanctioned by an official union.

You may eventually belong to the majority of the population that calls its partner either husband or wife, without truly understanding the complexity of the situation one has become entangled in. Such a relationship is important when it comes to raising children, but as far as other aspects go, it is purely a facade required by the legal and economic system. The strange thing is that rivers of ink are written on the topic, laws are enacted, demonstrations are held, the debates are ongoing. Men and women get married as soon as possible, and then get divorced—this is deeply rooted in tradition, with one sole aim: to produce children.

There are also men who want to marry other men and women who want to marry other women—and then get divorced. The problems, of course, do not necessarily stop here. One day some new program will be found to provide the mass media their daily bread and create embarrassment for legislators—such as marriages between various species of animals and humans, or worse yet, applying the concept of marriage to the free world of mating in wild animals.

All this waste of energy for a banal contract that

must regulate individual interests and financial relations. Wouldn't it be better to call it simply an agreement between two parties? Like all agreements, it will leave room for possible modifications, since, as far as we know, nothing is definitive on this earth. Perhaps not even death.

~~~

Albert had once been married. He often thought about the reasons he'd gotten married, why he'd done it. Television often showed debates, demonstrations and events that examined the demand for gay marriage. He asked himself why, but couldn't find an answer. The whole thing looked like a farce, a spectacle of sanctimony put on by a group which ironically defined itself as liberal and progressive. In reality, it represented a refusal by this group to seek to adapt a more modern vision to our social realm.

An absolute lack of imagination in creating new rules with new definitions and new names to describe a new type of relationship?

Albert thought that being gay, or a playboy, or just a "regular" type, or even a whore, was a person's own business. It was not up to others to judge, but at the same time each individual should not wave in the face of everyone else all his own habits only just to feel different or to make others feel different. What does it mean to go around wearing a T-shirt that says, *I'm gay* or *I'm a gourmet* or *I'm a fucker* or *I'm a drunk* or *I'm a golfer*, and so on?

Ah, who cares? Let them do what they want! The universe is big!

~~~

One thing he did know—that the memory of his marriage was burdensome, even if for him it had had no true legal basis. It was a bond beyond the law. It was a thought, an intuition, a part of life, a simple contact between souls. It was a convergence and a clash of personalities. What did all that have to do with those banal words, husband and wife?

They had first met in Japan, during a business trip. A large Japanese firm was seeking new financial solutions to boost its presence in international markets. It had called in consultants from various financial firms in order to put together a strategy. Albert found himself spending many hours with a representative from another American firm that operated in the same sector as his.

CHAPTER 5

Albert was walking not far from his home, on his way back from the restaurant where he'd had a good plate of fish and a decent glass of wine. He'd lunched alone. The atmosphere had been light and cheery, and the food had made him as peaceful as the clear, tepid day that surrounded him.

As he drew near his building, Marianne's face came to mind. It shone before his eyes. He distinctly saw her light brown, slightly wavy hair that brushed against her shoulders and framed her long, sharply angled face and its beautiful features—features that were so marked that her face seemed carved in wood. All except her nose, which was very normal and well joined, softer and shapelier than her cheekbones and chin. He stopped to gaze into his dream, at her eyes, green and incisive. He had been struck by her eyes in Japan. How they stood out amid thousands of pairs of black eyes! He seemed to be able to once again join arms with her, and with that sensation he set out for the marina, which was not far.

Marina Jack lies in the shadow of Sarasota's downtown high-rise condominiums. Its waters are protected by a peninsula with trees and fields, on the tip of which there is a fountain with bronze dolphins depicted leaping out of the water. Albert sat down on a bench near the fountain and was soon talking to Marianne—not in Tokyo, where they had first met, but in New York, where they had spent most of their time together.

In reality, they had never spent long periods of time together. They both worked, traveled. Both were caught up in a whirlwind of commitments. Both were ambitious and career-oriented.

But what did career-oriented actually mean?

What kind of career was it?

Those questions were never asked back then. Such a lifestyle seemed like the only option available.

Things might have been easier if neither of them had begun to let their thoughts stray and ask themselves some basic questions.

From that bench, he now found himself in New

York. They were getting out of a cab and he took her by the hand. The sky was already dark, but the city lights brightened everything else. Sometimes in these huge cities, one forgets the sky exists at all, to the point where the word sky takes on an almost poetic connotation, a word from days gone by.

That evening, for no particular reason, Albert lifted his eyes in search of the sky.

He halted for a moment.

Marianne tugged his hand. She had no idea why he had stopped. Had it perhaps been a premonition, or just a coincidence? Why was he recalling that moment so clearly today?

They began walking again. After just a few steps, they were entering a very cozy and well-lit restaurant. The place gave one the feeling of being wrapped in an suffused and warm atmosphere. The tables were set up in such a way as to guarantee privacy to each group of guests. Albert felt at ease. Marianne had discovered the place but this was their first time there. He wanted to ask her how she had found such a place or what personal experience had linked her to it.

Instinctively he had noted in Marianne's movements that there was something special in the air that evening. He figured he would hold his tongue and let himself be led along. In many cases that's always a wise thing to do anyway, especially when a woman shows a certain determination, whose cause is unknown or at least remote enough to keep you from moving on stable terrain.

Kicking off an important conversation or discussion between two people who physically and mentally belong to opposite sexes is always a potentially explosive situation, a minefield that's best to cross cautiously for the safety of both.

In reality, one of the main obstacles is perceiving the respective percentage of either sex present in each individual. It is highly improbable that an individual can be all man or all woman.

That night perhaps the sky wanted to let them know that this type of approach might be lived differently.

~~~

They read the menu with great care, to cover over a lull in the conversation and each one's need for intimacy. Something was in the air, but it eluded Albert. Their conversation resumed after they had ordered. It became more relaxed after their first glass of wine, but it still was not heading anywhere in particular. Then Marianne began talking about herself, and how she was feeling about work. She sunk her teeth into the subject with a determination that Albert had never seen in her .

In the past, Marianne, when not talking shop, had always been extremely pleasant, not in the least intense. She gave the impression of wanting to entertain herself and others, showing great desire to spend her free time happily. Albert also knew her more intimate moments. They had spent wonderful weekends together, and longer vacations as well. Sometimes just brief encounters after work, or dazzling evenings together, waking up the next morning in the same bed.

They talked about everything, and perhaps, now that he was reflecting upon the subject for the first time, they talked about nothing. They were just a couple of high finance professionals who spent a few pleasant hours together, joking about their experiences at work and trading ideas on the personalities of various characters that populated their lives. They told one another about past travels, talked politics, exchanged info on where to dine and the future of high finance, named the sports they were interested in, and reviewed the quick trips they had planned as an evasion from work-related tension.

The entire relationship, however, served as a framework for their professional lives—the heart of their existences.

Being at any rate human, which is to say, made up of spirit and body, lately they had discovered themselves touching each other more and more often, kissing. They spent more hours sitting together on the same couch, making love with intensity and noticed it when they were apart. But each of them always returned to the old routine, as if such moments were merely robbing time from duty. They hadn't understood that it was exactly the opposite. Those moments gave body to their lives; they provided support for their commitments.

That night Marianne was certain of this, let's say,

upside-down reality. She had been experiencing a sensation of incompleteness at work for some time, and all those limited arguments that particular world forces you to utter. Her professional encounters, which once thrilled her so, began to totally bore her. She felt like she was playing Monopoly. Human relationships were so cautious, calculated and careful as to eliminate that joy of complex scents that is born out of the communication of two things.

As the days went by, Marianne began to feel more and more detached from the people around her. She realized that most of her relationships, although they began pleasantly enough, were eventually damaged by a system of interacting that did not inspire or encourage emotional growth. Meanings were distorted, actions repeated, and communication stifled to the point where ideas were misperceived and intentions misjudged. Marianne desired authenticity; she was touched by a passion to discover the real essence that lies just below the surface of our everyday lives.

She began reading history books to see whether all this was a peculiarity of our times. She spoke to no one about it, not even Albert. She also read books on religious topics. She reread the Old and New Testaments with new eyes, different from when she had been taught from those books as a girl—and surely this new approach to reading the Old Testament left her forlorn. In Marianne's reasoning, problems regarding the economy, politics and relations among the official religions—which unfortunately wield much influence over politics and the economy—now took a back seat. She read and reasoned, even if she had no clear idea what "for herself" actually meant.

This new experience of hers had not yet brought her to understand that what she was going through was precisely that moment in which one begins to realize that yes, I am alone, surrounded by a small, haggard group of individuals. The rest is but a giant cauldron where everyone is trying to tell you what they want, with the goal of convincing you of something.

She spent hours studying history, which unfolded before her eyes with objectives and results that were almost always identical, except that they occurred at different times and in different places, in different languages, with different customs, clothing and colors. Her perfectly planned-out life as a businesswoman had lost its attraction. A process bigger than herself began corroding her spirit. Her profound sensitivity as a woman poked through the surface like a drowsy but determined current that spews the sea's waves into a strait studded with shoals.

This upheaval had been a long time coming; her tried and tested professionalism had kept it hidden and under control. Albert himself, so caught up in his abstract and superficial world of work, would never have guessed it. He was light years away from a state of mind such as hers. Had Marianne tried to expose her doubts to him that evening, more than likely Albert would have had the feeling of being struck by lightning on a clear, sunny day. Who knows how long it would have taken him to digest it all, or even just to sift through it all? Was there any hope of him ever sharing her feelings?

~~~

Marianne reached across the table as if to invite Albert to take her hand. Lately, they'd often held hands. Her face was brightly colored and showed an intense expression. She had already spoken much that evening, and indeed broached the topic of the utility of the lives they led. She revealed a certain discomfort regarding work. Albert interpreted this outburst as a sign of exhaustion. At any rate, he had noticed that she'd seemed less dedicated to work of late, or at least she spoke less about it. Then again, being consummate professionals who did basically the same things in different organizations, they had never shared the day-to-day details of their jobs, unless they happened to be involved in the same operation, as was the case when they'd first met in Japan. Albert was not privy to her daily routine. He knew only that she earned a lot of money and that her life was considered a success. Their relationship was going smoothly, at least on the surface, inasmuch as two persons with two very independent lives could hope for. They took pleasure in seeing one another. Going out together was a good release for both of them. Making love and seeking diversion in the needs of each other's bodies and their mutual fantasies proved effective medicine against stress.

Albert took her hand and looked into her eyes with a certain apprehension. Perhaps she had bad news to tell him. Her eyes were serious, but at the same time gave off strong intensity and seemed to want to communicate that her mind was alert. With a soft, sweet tone Marianne resumed the monologue that she had just broken off from.

"As I was saying, I think society today forgets that there are reasons why people and things have different roles in life. We make life more complicated by insisting that everything is equal. People change the meanings of words from the way they're defined in dictionaries. But tonight I have decided to use this modern way of thinking without asking myself whether I agree with it or not.

"It's pretty much considered normal that there no longer exists a difference in roles or states of mind between men and women, or among whites, blacks, yellows, and so on, or Gentiles and Jews, or Chinese, Europeans, Africans, Americans... My job, my life—they're very similar to yours. They run parallel. Maybe the only place we realize that we belong to opposite sexes is in bed.

"But we're not in bed now, so I've decided to play what was traditionally considered the male role. Will you marry me?"

Albert gazed at her, his eyes popping, though he remained perfectly still and did not say a word. Even his hand in Marianne's made not the slightest movement. His fingers continued to exert the same pressure they had exerted a moment earlier. It was as if he did not wish to show any kind of reaction that he might later regret.

Marianne went on.

"I've reached a point in my life where I've begun to wonder whether it's time to get back to basics. With every day that passes, I feel more and more like a woman. And I keep asking myself whether this is a good thing or a bad thing. I've been reading a lot. Reading and thinking. I've been comparing my life to other women's lives—women of our time, women of the past.

"Can it be possible that most of the values we've been basing our lives on are so obsolete? Deep down, what kind of woman am I? Super active and devoted exclusively to business? Or is there something else I want? I don't know. I've been molded and taught to act in a way that seemed perfectly natural to me, but in reality I'm just a product of the system.

"You see, I'd like to learn about the other side of the coin. I don't exactly know which side, because in truth there are many sides. All I know is, I've got to get out of this stereotyped world.

"Do you have to be in love to get married? Or does love come afterward? All I know is that I like being with you and lately I think of you often. Let's get married and see if it enriches our lives.

"Come on, we're business people, we're used to modifying our decisions based on necessity. If it doesn't work out, we'll get divorced. We'll do a prenuptial agreement, that way there will be no haggling, no bickering, everything will be easy and settled beforehand. It doesn't sound very romantic, but I think that for us, or at least for me, the road to romance is just beginning.

"Well, say something!

"Is what I'm saying stupid? Am I insulting you? Or do you think this thing is possible?

"Aren't you a little romantic too, way deep down inside? I think you are, I've read it in your eyes and on your skin when we hold and caress one another. Or is it just sex and nothing more?"

She had rambled on without a pause, but had given Albert time to control his reactions.

He put up a very formal smile as if he were conducting a business deal. Caressing her hand, he answered, "If you think this is the way to go, then let's let the idea grow inside us for a few days. You're very precious to me, and sometimes your intelligence even puts mine to shame. Let's pay up and go back to your place to digest this all."

He was good at convincing people, good at dowsing the flames. He had built a solid career on these qualities.

To avoid any squabbles, most times they split the check. That night, however, Marianne picked up the tab. She had already been acting out the traditional male role and would continue to do so until her femininity, which she felt growing inside her each day, told her to do otherwise.

CHAPTER 6

Albert rose from the bench in the tiny park at the edge of the peninsula that separated the marina from Sarasota Bay. He gazed at the trees. On one pandemonium seemed to have broken out. A fairly large group of green parakeets had just arrived. It was as though they were talking, or better, arguing with one another. They fluttered from one branch to the next, and then back to the branch they had just left. It was total chaos, yet the scene was bursting with life. Suddenly, just as they had arrived, the group of small green birds took off again with the same determination, like a swarm of bees. They left the park, following the cries of other birds.

When it came down to it, what had happened that night at the restaurant in New York might have been completely normal, even if slightly out of the ordinary. Actually, that was only the start of a series of events that rocked Albert's well-organized life and led him into direct contact with the drama that human existence often has in store for us.

Now, as he walked slowly home, his eyes still saw Marianne's face, still picked up on the intensity that it gave off that night at the restaurant.

He went up to his apartment and sat down at his desk in order to better fix in his memory those moments of the past that had such an impact on his life—moments which would eventually lead him to begin a whole new life for himself right there in Sarasota.

Actually, he never quite got a handle on everything that had happened. He decided to jot down a few notes, like in a diary, to outline the change that he experienced. He had to get it set in his mind why before he never would have even remotely considered stopping to sit on a park bench to watch a group of quarrelsome parakeets, much less get a kick out of it.

Marianne had infected him with a virus that acted slowly but relentlessly, hounding him without respite. But really it was a soft, sweet illness—though rife with regret and laced with profound sadness.

It might have seemed as if he'd been bitten by the classic love bug, only this was much more; it was an existential malady. Indeed, his raison d'etre was up for grabs every day. Every day he would be forced to deal with the reality of the practical world and the desire to do something truly wonderful and worthwhile—though he did not know what this something was, and by himself could never have figured it out. He took paper and pen. For a moment, his top and bottom eyelids nearly met.

~~~

He was back at Marianne's place, sitting on the couch in her living room, where they had gone after leaving the restaurant. She had already emptied herself. She seemed another woman, sweet and almost yielding. She had gotten out everything that was bottled up inside her. She had also asked a very important question without receiving a definite answer. The businesswoman poised to react and get around any obstacle that came her way seemed to have disappeared. She was now sipping good 18-year-old scotch in silence.

Albert was confused and felt somewhat ill at ease. He, too, was beginning to understand that in this world there exist languid moments and that they are contagious. At such times, reason serves no more; it is best to give the brain a break and let yourself live.

Back then Albert was not yet able to completely

understand all this. His intuition hinted at something, but because he was moving in what to him was unfamiliar territory, he paid close attention to what he said and how he acted. He did have the feeling, however, that he was behaving a little clumsily. She broke the ice by putting an arm around his neck and leaning her cheek on his. Upon contact, Marianne's skin gave the impression of being even softer than usual, and her spirit more compliant than usual. It seemed as though she expected something from him. Albert interpreted her move as he pleased, which is to say, he gave it the classic male-suddenly-turned-on interpretation. Albert's subsequent proposal proved a way out that both could accept. Then they would see.

~~~

A weekend like that isn't easy to forget. They spent it holed up inside four walls in search of themselves, in search of their own intimacy, while the city went on buzzing outside. Albert could still to this day feel it under his skin, and he found himself shedding a few tears. He didn't know whether they were tears of joy or immense pain. After all, those fleeting moments belonged to the past and had been buried in time.

Sunday night he slept back at his place. Monday the rat race recommenced. Tuesday he flew to Atlanta. He took advantage of the following Sunday to hop a flight to São Paulo, Brazil. His business engagements practically provided an excuse for taking a breather in order to snap out of that unusual parenthesis he'd just experienced. All too often work becomes an excuse to shun the unsettling questions on how one relates to humanity. Yes, his job was a strong, steadfast alibi. It was only once he'd gotten to Brazil that he realized he hadn't called Marianne. He should have felt guilty, but he skipped over that thought. Anyway, Marianne had known he was going. It was still a stupid excuse—as if cell phones had never been invented.

She didn't call either. She worked, but unenthusiastically. Within her, the patience of her womanly being was getting the best of that typical businesswoman's craving to get the facts and wrap things up as quickly as possible. Her thoughts were adrift and distant from everything and everybody.

She was alone with herself.

After two weeks she took some time off and went to visit friends—a couple with a large house on the shore, in Sarasota. She bought another cell with a new number and ordered her secretary to give it out to no one. She left her old cell phone turned off, with the message that said to call her office for information.

Albert's future was being plotted out unbeknownst to him—unbeknownst to both of them, actually.

In Sarasota, Marianne had the time to better assess her frame of mind. She spent hours talking it over with her friends and trying to sort things out.

She also took time to have some fun—sunbathing, boating, playing tennis, going to the theater. One friend even taught her how to prepare a few delicious dishes, and Marianne found that she felt less and less like eating out all the time. She had been in the habit of taking her meals at restaurants, or eating takeout food from the neighborhood deli.

Albert was present in her subconscious. Sometimes she thought of her marriage proposal, wondering whether she still wanted to go through with it. More than likely she had just been confused and needed Albert to bring her back to reality. Perhaps he had remained distant, isolated in his world.

But what was his real world?

What was her real world?

Financially, things were looking good for her. She was in the process of closing a few deals that required very little of her time and would guarantee substantial earnings for at least two years. She braced herself. She called her firm, flew to New York and returned with a contract that gave her six months leave of absence—time enough to dedicate to herself.

All she had to do was to maintain professional relations and keep an eye on a couple of situations that needed defining—things she could easily take care of over the phone or via email. In six months she would return to work and get back to the old grind. She also knew that in her field there was a high rate of attrition. A long absence could turn into a permanent one, because in the meantime others were pushing their way ahead, moving, plotting.

But Marianne was young and sure of herself. She decided to risk it.

~~~

One thing she'd already obtained— she'd disappeared from Albert's life with the determination that only women possess. Not that they never talked over the phone. They chatted once in a while, Albert at times chatting a bit too much, though she always knew how to wiggle her way out of any subject and give the impression that she was like perfectly transparent glass which disturbs the view in no way at all. Though, at the same time, that glass doesn't add much to the view, either.

SUNSET IN SARASOTA

CHAPTER 7

Albert relived these past experiences as if watching a film. He couldn't sit still in his seat. He recalled phone calls, his embarrassment at not being able to understand what was happening, the changes in Marianne's mood and how he felt he had no other choice but to seek refuge in his work.

He got up, poured himself a scotch and water on the rocks, and went to the window to sip it. Outside it was already dark. He had to get away from the mass of memories that assailed him, even if for him they had become a reason for living. Life, however, is meant to be lived with actions and not merely in dreams and reminiscence. Lately this concept occupied more and more of his thoughts. Would he have to make a clean break altogether from his past? How could this be done?

For now it was better to focus on something truly concrete, like going out for dinner, possibly with someone. He tried calling Greg and Joy, a strange couple he'd been seeing a lot of lately. They lived together but were not married. They didn't seem all that close to one another, either. The difference in their character gave one the impression that they were a mismatched couple. Albert knew very little of them and their experiences, much less how they led their lives. He worked in real estate, probably a broker, though it seemed to Albert that in that part of the world most people had a real estate license. She painted, or at least said she did, though she never spoke of her work.

The two were cheerful and pleasant. You could talk about anything with them, or nothing. Spending a few hours with them was easy, especially sitting in a restaurant.

Greg was always up on what was happening in Sarasota and the surrounding area, and spoke with a sharp sense of humor. Hearing the local gossip made Albert feel less isolated in his new reality. Joy was more taciturn. She was a keen observer, and the few comments she made were usually on the money. She gave the impression of enjoying her existence, as if during the day she was able to store up so much strength and serenity from the Florida sun or from her painting, which she would then distribute to others over the course of an evening.

"If you've got nothing better to do, how about grabbing some dinner at our favorite restaurant? I feel rich tonight; it's on me."

An hour later they were sitting at a table talking and laughing, and like everyone, playing that old game of watching and being watched.

That evening he discovered many things.

Storms in Florida arrive suddenly, bearing lightning and thunder, white clouds, black clouds and gray clouds, and water, lots of water, as if a river were cascading out of the sky and drenching all around. And just like a Florida storm, only minutes after arriving at the restaurant the couple erupted into such an out-of-control argument that it seemed Mother Nature herself had unchained all her wrath and fury. Albert felt embarrassed and excluded. No matter how hard he tried, he was unable to understand the reasons for this disagreement. He didn't have a clue. Their battle raged like water crashing down from the sky, directionless and with no precisely identifiable source.

Greg's features hardened all at once. At first he spoke excitedly, not very rationally. Then he grew more careful and exact in his reasoning; his confused rage became confrontational dictated by rancor that bordered on viciousness. For her part, Joy's replies were not overly coherent. She seemed to be overwhelmed by his stubborn insistence.

At this point it was apparently a senseless argument. Accusations were being leveled. Their respective mindsets, their divergent ways of looking at life, were being challenged. Greg was the "salesman" — he thought he could convince anybody of anything, and this translated into income and survival. Joy, on the other hand, was the woman who took on life in a straightforward manner. She believed in relationships, in art. She longed for someone who loved her paintings, her spirit, but most of all, someone who loved her pleasant femininity — which was the only way she could have known true happiness and understand the reason for her existence. After three years of living together, a few basic initial errors had mushroomed into a lacerating disparity and an inevitable clash.

~~~

Albert wondered why they had to pick tonight, in his presence, to battle it out. Was this some sort of mystical trick being played on him by Marianne? Was this spectacle of unhappiness a lesson for him to reflect upon the restrictive parameters of relationships? To remind him that his soul was, ultimately, free? Was Marianne helping him learn to appreciate that not everything in this world has to do with work, obligations or professional conduct? He felt Marianne's presence — and the joy and illumination that came with feeling her near him. There is something inside us that does not reason, something that lives a life apart, within its own confines and dreams of creation, whether or not such dreams come true.

~~~

Very calmly, Joy rose from her seat and left the restaurant. Albert watched her from the window as she walked down the street. She was crying, though still with great dignity. Then he said simply, "Greg, there's not much left for me to do but pay the check and call it a night—like I said, it's on me tonight. You go catch up with her and take her home. Stuff like this happens all the time with couples. If you don't mind, I'll finish my dessert and the wine."

Greg did not answer. He was livid. His useless man's pride had taken a pretty hard blow. The fact was, she had gotten up calmly and left as if his words had been rain in a Florida storm—violent but brief, with some of its water being absorbed by the land, but most running off and winding up in the ocean. Then its clear skies, the land and its inhabitants—men and women, animals and plants—have other things to do. They keep growing and flying and walking down their road.

Albert finished his dessert by himself. For the first time in many years he felt as if he were together with Marianne, who spoke to him. "See what I was trying to tell you? Don't waste any more time. Free your spirit and your body. They live in symbiosis. They also need maintenance."

~~~

He recalled having read something to that effect in a book, which tried to define love and sex as a mutual and innocent exchange of fantasies and energies that reassures us that we are the product of a fusion of body and spirit, and that both require maintenance. He realized it was not Marianne's voice that was reminding him of this, but the virus that she had transmitted to him. And that virus was growing inside him.

CHAPTER 8

That night he couldn't manage to fall asleep. He'd learned that you can't let time pass you by, filled with only memories, distractions, conversations with friends, social engagements. He decided he had to act. It was time to get back to work.

When it came down to it, having to work for a living was a great invention. Sure, it was sometimes a bitter pill to swallow, but without money and the systems that revolved around it, the world would be controlled only by gigantic brawls and vaudeville shows - an even more tragicomic situation than it already is. Give a man peace and quiet and a little power, and goodness knows what he'll be capable of inventing! We'd have a bunch of Saddam Husseins on the loose, big or small, ready for anything in order to stave off boredom. Others would be able to adjust to any sad situation that presented itself—anything, as long as it provided a reason to survive—while they plotted revenge, that, alas, might never arrive.

The invention of money was a brilliant idea. Money is something so impersonal that, in truth, it means nothing.

You can't eat money, can you? Can you have fun looking at it? Touching it?

Well, maybe someone who suffered from a bad case of greed and stinginess could! If you don't use money, you'll soon realize that money itself is quite boring, and that you'll need to come up with another excuse for your life. Sure, that excuse might turn out to be something wonderful and good, but the danger is, it might also turn out to be something unhealthy for you and those around you.

Today, we take it pretty much for granted that our security depends on a home and money. The former represents a real need—perhaps that's why we call it real estate. We're not built to live naked in the wilderness. But in and of itself, money—if we scrutinize the concept—is really quite useless. Imagine if the system were to suddenly change. For example, we conclude that aluminum is worth more than gold, and that money should be made out of ceramic and not paper.

In truth, "turbulence" great and small occurs much more frequently than people believe. Just think of all the times man has sought changes in political science and economics. Take communism, for instance; or the devaluation of currencies; sector crises; the fluctuating value of labor. Should you dedicate a few minutes of your day to such assessments, you're likely to meet up with anxiety and apprehension. If you're lucky, though, one thing you will understand—and this is the most important aspect of our existences—that nothing is guaranteed, and that we're on this earth to give, not to receive. So... let us give with great cheer. Because there's no escape from it, sooner or later our very nature itself, our most essential self will demand a final report on our lives, a summing up, and at that point we risk becoming our own worst enemies.

How foolish to believe that a system can guarantee us all we need. It would be more honest to simply say, the system tries to do its best to assure you a happy future, but you, you must be the first to think of yourself and contribute to the well-being of the system through your commitment. In this way, perhaps we may actually keep functioning longer. The key thing here is the "longer" part.

~~~

The truth is that every system or civilization has a time limit that we tend to ignore, and we end up swimming in an unknown sea, thinking how wonderful the beach back there was.

Will we ever find that beach again? That depends on many factors, including so-called good luck, or as Christians call it, Providence. At any rate, the longer you're able to keep swimming, the better your chances of finding that beach again. A lot of it depends on our sheer willpower.

~~~

For the moment Albert had no need to work. The administration of his investments took no more than a few hours a week: everything was done on the internet. He traded dollars for euros, and then back again. He took advantage of the opportunities that the capitalist system makes available. It's basically a good system, but if you don't watch out, you may suddenly become prey to its negative, and even dangerous sides.

One must live within the system, contribute to it, otherwise the system itself will crush you—either by taking away money you have earned, or by giving you more—so much money, in fact, that you risk merely admiring it. In the latter scenario, such sums may be useless if your life lacks passions, or even lethal because you have allowed the sense of their importance to grow within you, practically deceiving yourself into believing money is a living being with which to entertain a relationship.

Money represents but one aspect of the system, with all its defects and dangers.

He remembered his father telling him, "Your

life revolves around your job, so you've got to do what you know best. Choose a job that's useful to the world. Be active in the world you live in, and make it known that you're always striving to improve your skills, whatever they are—whether you become a manager, a doctor, a salesman or someone who cleans offices. There are no first- or second-class jobs, whatever the job, as long as you do it well, as long as you're a consummate professional. And remember—if you want something special to happen, you've got to play an active role in society.

"The trains go by, but if you don't show up at the station you cannot take one of them, not even the slowest."

Albert nodded. "True, true... I have to work and deal concretely with people. I'm still young and I have to put myself to the test, commit myself, abandon the idea that I exist only to think. Thinking too much can be fatal for men, as long as we walk the earth."

~~~

Sarasota seemed to be growing before one's very eyes. New buildings sprung up everywhere, as did new clusters of buildings in the county, shopping centers, homes and all that the development of an area brings with it. He got in his car and drove around to familiarize himself with what was going on and to perhaps better understand the needs of the community. Maybe he could find a piece of land to build on. Maybe the project would be a success.

The financial end was no problem for him, in that he possessed the necessary capital and had experience in managing it. The question was, however, would he be able to manage all the complications that arise when actually attempting to build something? This he had no experience in at all. He had always limited himself to setting goals and juggling numbers, assessing the market and men.

He would have to live up to the challenge of regaining his self-respect and feeling like other people. He would have to hunker down and dedicate his energies to the system in order to avoid embarrassing questions he might ask himself, and postpone answering these questions for the time being.

He had to get back to work, get back to practical problems. He would concern himself with sticking to his commitments. His new life would require scheduling, deadlines, to keep everything running smoothly, at a faster pace.

He had to quit seeking refuge in the memory of Marianne. He had to stop continuously reliving the contradictions of their relationship—a relationship that had been buoyed up by their common search for inner growth and development. Now he searched alone, led on by the example set for him by Marianne, for she was no longer there to help him.

He had to catch the train that would take him to the next station and keep his life running to the steady, intense rhythm of the wheels rattling along the rails of existence.

CHAPTER 9

It seemed as though everyone in Sarasota had been taken up by the building craze. He decided to join them. A few months later he was co-owner of a beautiful piece of land out in the county, in partnership with an architect friend of his. The project they had in mind consisted of a residential complex—nothing huge—and a small shopping area, a so-called mixed-use arrangement.

Most projects begin with big ideas fueled by enthusiasm, vision and creative inspiration. Those used to the process know how frequently creativity has to be muted to follow the boring requests of the market and the bureaucracy of the system in place. Albert understood all too well that an idea born of brilliance can be watered down to become a mediocre reality. Dreams are put aside in the name of somber functionality; elegance forsaken to save a dollar. One day you find yourself facing that haunting question: "Will it still work?"

New visions, great and small, are the terror of mankind. Better to buy a mechanical Rolex chronograph, even if everyone knows it doesn't keep the exact time, because the important thing is that it's a Rolex, which has potential value in itself. Of course, no one knows what good this potential value actually is. Then there are those ultra-thin quartz watches that are incredibly accurate, the ones so light and sleek you hardly realize you're wearing one. They are surely a marvel of technology and design, but fashion is a whole other ballgame—irrational, blind and allergic to new things that make sense.

This is how his first experience as an entrepreneur shaped up. Time took flight once again, began consuming itself. This was positive as far as Albert's situation went, though soon he would come face to face with an unpleasant reality spiked with outrageous snags and delays. One thing is knowing that bureaucracy exists, and that it doesn't work very well. But when you meet up with it in person, to survive you can take it in either of two different ways. The first, and perhaps the best, is to live out the experience with irony. It's like being at the circus, watching the clowns perform—if they're really good, you split your sides laughing. The second attitude possible is to reason things out calmly, trying to understand why certain obstacles have arisen. Over-insisting on the second method, however, is likely to drive you crazy.

At that moment in time, Sarasota County was going through a sharp phase of "negative efficiency," to put it politely. The heart of the problem lay in the climate that ruled throughout the various offices: practically incomprehensible. Most of the officials were good people, just caught up in the system. The commissioners did not officially approve of this system, but spoke of it as if in reality it wasn't so negative. After all, they were politicians; they expressed only concepts and were not running the day-to-day operations. Someone else would have to put those concepts into practice.

This attitude seemed to be an illness spread worldwide. Perhaps it is dictated by a mania for grandeur on the part of some people at the head of the system who envision the expansion of bureaucracy as a healthy and necessary growth of the government as a corporation with an ever-increasing number of employees. Too bad these people missed one very important fact: a corporation of this type generates only costs and doesn't produce any wealth.

Worse, the system places less importance on human ingenuity than on computer results, which are easy to control by just changing one factor. Even the most cooperative bureaucrat—and there are many—relies on software programs and computer technology to explore the parameters of potential projects rather than on his own power of thinking. "The computer model shows us," they say, and "the computer model doesn't allow for..." Then again, perhaps it was merely the application of the universal "no" theory, according to which, if you don't say no, you're gripped by the fear that no one will realize you even exist.

In the end, though, Albert realized that the system was ultimately a fair one. Bureaucrats, after all, are entitled to follow the system in place; it's up to those who deal with them to learn how to navigate this system.

Albert now found himself a victim of the same tricks he used to use when he thought he could lead the real world from a Wall Street office by deciding goals and indicating rules and strategies. The world sure looks different from the other side, where real people live and have to produce things so that the world can keep turning, living, prospering and criticizing.

~~~

Albert had asked Joy to help him with the interior decorating on the project and met frequently with her. He didn't want Greg as his sales agent, however, since Greg inspired a feeling of distrust in him. The two of them still shared the same house, because it was easier that way, but at the same time they were drifting further and further apart. Joy, absorbed in a wave of artistic fervor, spent most of her time in her studio, and when she wasn't there she was out promoting her paintings. For his part, Greg had become more and more obsessed with finding ways to make lots of money fast. Like many people bent on easy earnings, success seemed further out of reach each day, leaving a trail of bitterness and frustration. The two slept in separate rooms, and only rarely had sex—more out of habit, or need, than for the joy of being together.

It was inevitable that two people like Albert and Joy—two people, as it were, hobbling through life, though longing to discover new roads—would wind up in bed together. The bed helps people to share their uncertainties with one another, to speak softly of things to be remembered, and those to be forgotten, and those to aim for.

It happened at his house.

They had decided to have lunch together, something quick. He had some excellent smoked salmon. They also drank a bottle of white wine—something they never did at noontime.

It was a lovely day, if a tad too warm. The air conditioning inside his apartment spurred them to drink that wine down, which brought the heat of the sun to their souls. The sun melted the fog, infused a desire to live in them, to communicate, to sing, to love—whether true love or the fleeting kind in search of intense contact to communicate through actions and not words.

After his experience with Marianne, Albert had realized how important sex was for both bodily and spiritual peace. He had had other women, but only she had inspired grand and lasting emotions in him. Marianne was still in his thoughts, still in his heart, still in his dreams. But time transforms passions into impalpable memories. So when he found Joy completely naked in his arms, he felt invigorated anew, from the tips of his toes to the end of each hair.

She was soft, with soft features and two beautiful natural breasts that seemed to press insistently against every part of Albert's body. Her hands had a delicate touch, her legs were lean and slithered over the sheets with a slow, sinuous movement. Albert figured it would take all his sensitivity to satisfy her, and she deserved it.

As the hours passed it became an obsession for him, a commitment—though he never realized the real reason for it—which came from his spirit's most essential core. Perhaps he felt a new and profound relationship blossoming with a creature who gave the impression of being so simple and real—attributes that always go hand in hand with intelligence. This was the best afternoon he had spent since Marianne had left him, and since he had left his job on Wall Street a short while after that.

~~~

He had a new job, a real commitment, and perhaps a new woman able to help lift him out of the apathy he had become stuck in. That night when he went to bed he could still smell Joy's scent there. Turning in his sleep, he had the sensation of bumping against her breasts, of fondling her intimate zones. He had never experienced anything of the sort, yet he had slept with other women after Marianne had left him. Actually, he still did not understand whether or not she was gone forever.

Time is of this earth, life comes from afar and love barely grazes these concepts.

That night he slept very little, in bits and pieces.

"Marianne, help me…let me find what you taught me to appreciate."

CHAPTER 10

Albert's life seemed to be entering a new phase, more concrete and common to many mortals. He would have to make his own business grow, deal with suppliers, bureaucrats, bankers, accountants, lawyers, clients. He discovered that large companies keep these sectors well separated from one another. How could an accountant and a salesman ever understand another? In the past he hadn't cared much about this. It was up to the others to invent rules and make them work.

At his new little company everything was handled by a few people within the space of not many square feet, where it was up to him, Albert, as their boss and the man in charge, to maintain order and harmony, and make that forced cohabitation more bearable and, preferably, pleasant. He was the boss. He was the problem-solver, he always had the last word. He found out that having the last word in this kind of work was not an easy position to be in because jeopardizing the initial idea of the project and putting the investment at risk, along with the people involved in the job, can happen all too easily.

Up until now he had only been a "numbers boss." Behind those numbers were people working or investors hoping, but for him it was only just a question of numbers, and he had no close bonds with them. Today, however, he was in charge of everything, directly exposing himself, ready for victory or shipwreck. What a strange and new sensation! At any rate, it provided him with a perception of real life.

Sales were not going well, or at least they were below the forecast. He had already spent more money than he had figured. And that damned bureaucracy seemed to be out to get him! In reality, of course, bureaucracy was just an expensive, stupid game that everybody had to play. Some survived, others did not. After a while, Albert learned that if you asked for what was right, in the end you usually got it. It was necessary to take into account lengthy procedures, lawyers, consultants, and absurd delays that Albert never seemed to understand the reasons for. Back on Wall Street it had been so easy to draw up a budget and wait for everything to be carried out as planned. Why did he now have to go through a bunch of useless hitches to achieve results which, most of the time, were pretty much taken for granted from the start? The answer seemed so simple to him. A lot of people were living off that project.

Back in the old days, the powerful and the Mafia extorted people, whereas today the system did it legally. In one way or another, the people always end up paying. The methods used today were just more sophisticated. And basically, the world has always worked this way. Generations of priests and preachers had lived by tricking the people and then providing solutions. They invented the Holy Inquisition, making use of an ingenious idea: "You must love and respect the Creator and act accordingly." Who could contradict a statement like that? It was right and good. What was not right and good were the aims and methods applied.

Thus Albert was able to understand the so-called ecologists.

Everybody loves nature, everybody wants a greener world, better air. But like the Holy Inquisition, such a wonderful idea was abused to create power and positions that were a boon to a lot of people. Once he found this out, he felt more at ease. There exists the right to work for your own interests, to try and create for yourself an occupation in line with the skills you possess. But why did this have to make other peoples' lives unbearable? What it came down to was that nature, plants and animals had become an excuse some people used to create power for themselves, to take the place of God, just as priests had done during the Holy Inquisition.

Any solution that might make sense was ditched right off the bat. Then problems would grow, ballooning to huge proportions, leading to mindless discussions, whose sole aim was, in reality, to justify the existence of that tiny piece of power that someone had tenaciously conquered. What should have been worked out in a few hours with three people took months and a slew of experts whose only joy in life was interpreting written rules.

This was as far from nature as the Inquisition was from Jesus. But both nature and Jesus were bothersome — they were too simple and practical.

Albert's brief contact with the "political-ecologists" was an experience so intense and draining that he decided to hand the matter over to other experts in the political-ecological realm who worked for him as consultants. He loved nature and all its creatures too much to be able to speculate on it. He also understood that there were compromises, which he was not able to formulate in the language of the self-defined experts. He limited himself to practically stuttering a few suggestions, while the experts on both sides poured out their detailed explanations with all manner of graphs and charts and print-outs and computers. Well then, creative jobs were contaminated by the same rules as Wall Street! Reality had no room for common sense. The game, though slightly different, cruder and more tangible, was laid out on the same basis.

It comforted him to think that now at least he

could see something rising up from the round, something he could touch, a true bit of wealth.

He talked about all this with Joy. They made love, talked and laughed. One day she showed up at Albert's and without any prelude whatsoever, said bluntly,

"I've rented an apartment. I left Greg."

Albert stared at her intensely.

Was there standing before him a true free woman, sweet and active, fearless and bent on living her own life?

Who said that the "knight in shining armor" had to be a man, anyway?

SUNSET IN SARASOTA

CHAPTER 11

Where was Marianne just then? Albert was sure
that no matter where she was, she would have ap-
proved of his new life and his relationship with Joy.
How could he talk to her, find her and ask her all
those questions that had been bubbling up inside
him?

Joy came to his place often; they dined together
almost every evening.

They took things day by day.

No plans, no plying each other with questions
about their respective past experiences. But with

time something began to find its way to the surface. Joy guessed that there remained a part of Albert's former love life that he was still very attached to. But why ruin their truly pleasant routine of dinners, work, talk and sex? She said nothing and he did not seem at all curious about her past. Indeed, he appreciated her fresh, forward-looking take on life. Yet Marianne's name worked its way unintentionally into several conversations, and one night while dreaming, Albert hugged Joy and uttered the other woman's name with great intensity.

Joy was not the jealous type, but she, like nearly all women, was curious. She didn't know how to approach the subject. Late one afternoon, while enjoying a cocktail together in her studio, Joy said, almost distractedly, "I'd like to do a portrait of Marianne, if you can describe her to me with precision. I feel like I owe it to you and that you want it."

He seemed zapped of strength. He opened his mouth repeatedly, then asked, "How did you know that Marianne was so important to me?"

"I don't know anything about it, just that you must have loved this woman, and that she left you with an indelible, beautiful memory!"

"You're right… but how'd you figure it out?"

"It didn't take a genius. You talk about her often enough. Brief mentions, but that name slips off your lips more often than it should. One night you were dreaming, and you hugged me with such tenderness as you spoke her name, as if you were thanking her for something. Then you woke up, smiled at me, then rolled over and fell back to sleep. I still wonder whether you recognized me at that moment..."

"Of course I recognized you, but I always asked myself whether I really said her name out loud or just imagined it. You were there, you gave me enormous comfort. I think I can love you. I've never told you so, but I think it's true. Marianne advised me to."

"Who is this Marianne anyway, and just how does she go about advising you on these matters? If you don't want to tell me, it doesn't matter. We can go out to eat and put it out of our minds."

"Marianne was my wife, but more than that she was the person who changed my life, even before I knew it!"

"Are you divorced?"

"No."

"Then why don't you invite her down to Sarasota?"

"Because I don't know where she is."

"But there must be a way to find her, today you can find out anything and everything about everybody. Or don't you want to find her? Maybe your memories are so nice that you don't want to face reality."

"I have no problem facing reality, only I don't know how."

"Look for her!"

"Where?"

"You must have some idea where she might be..."

"All I know is that her name is written on the monument where the Twin Towers used to be in

New York. She was there for an appointment on 9-11. And now her name's up there, clear and perfectly visible... where she is, I don't know. I don't know where I'm going, either, don't know where the world's going..."

~~~

Joy had the sensation that the light had disappeared from the room. She sat there, immobile. Then she took his hand and they sat there in silence, observing the darkness all around them—while in reality it was late afternoon in Sarasota, Florida, and light poured in through the open window.

CHAPTER 12

Now Albert had someone he could share his past with.

This was definitely a step ahead.

During the next few days he explained to Joy the basic highlights of his life, with episodes strung together as in a TV soap. She seemed to listen carefully. Hearing his story probably helped her to better understand Albert and fed her desire to get to know him even more.

In telling his story to Joy, Albert relived the period

of his life up till when Marianne took a six-month leave of absence from work in order to dedicate time to herself, away from him. In reality, the absence of Marianne from his life hadn't lasted years, the way it often happened in 19th-century romance novels.

The sensations and fixations of our time come and go quickly, as if they had adapted to the rhythm of television, news and fashion.

Today a decision is considered excellent and indispensable, tomorrow it is harshly criticized, after a week it is forgotten, and two months later it is re-implemented.

It's all part of such a superficial process, conditioned by the results of polls and guided by a never-ending barrage of news. It's necessary to print, to sell, to show that you've invented something, be it only a shirt with no collar—just to get mankind to change styles and rake in the dough. Of course, it doesn't always work out that way. The wind changes directions and the old shirts are back in style, so are the cars that look more like the ones we adored when we were young.

The pendulum swings quickly back to its original position. And though it remains but briefly, it is sure to return.

~~~

Thus, only six months later Marianne was back to the same old grind in New York, and back together with Albert. But their spirits had changed, they could no longer so thoroughly identify with the decadent, so-called New York international multiculturalism, where all too often the only idol is money and what it can buy. Where giving your word doesn't count, where arrogance infuses art, politics, furnishings, hobbies, the choice of a restaurant and drawing-room conversation.

They slowly realized that they were each experiencing a transformation of sorts: a need to break free from the superficial fabric of their lives, even if they perceived this change at different levels of intensity.

Whenever he happened to catch the daily closing of the Stock Exchange on TV in the evening, and witnessed the ceremony in which a group applauds from a balcony while one individual among them strikes with the official hammer to mark the end of that day's trading on Wall Street, Albert would say to himself, "Look how those oversized kids like to play I'm-a-big-man. They move lots of money around, even if it's only on computers. They try to be slick, try to be tricky, holding up a world that's floating in the void. Strange…come to think of it, even planet earth is floating in the void! Lots of money, lots of slick tricks, lots of Mr. Grassos, lots of compromises, and then…the void!"

~~~

The seed planted by Marianne had definitely taken root. Oddly enough, it rocked Albert more than it shook Marianne, though this might be considered normal. After all, women are often quick to pick up on big changes, yet maintain a profound sense of reality in their attempt to bridle violent developments in themselves, and avoid sudden disasters. Men sometimes like to play the knight in shining armor who aggressively pursues, without a second thought, the ideas that have influenced them. An exception must surely be made for the so-called "fanatical" women, often intimidated by the male condition that they themselves are secretly envious of. These women are always ready to foment, with admirable determination, complications and useless friction.

Marianne, whose maturity left her well beyond such women who were unable to evolve, had returned to work with a somewhat detached air, going about her tasks without the enthusiasm she once showed, but with resigned professionalism.

For his part, Albert had become a disobedient child. He worked, but was like a lion in a cage. He never missed a chance to criticize and at times made himself unpleasant. At the same time, a sense of dependence was growing inside him towards the woman who had opened his eyes to the meaning of life.

It had only been an initiation, if only because his teacher still did not have such clear ideas herself. Although who's really got clear ideas, anyway? The world is made up of just questions and timid replies, if any replies at all. He'd learned this at least. He was no longer sure that the sole important thing was, for example, to produce the cheapest shoes in China, and sell them in wealthy markets, and trigger a mechanism that worked at least for a while, until it's time to pass the hot potato to someone else, after, of course, having gotten rich off it. It's not that it was wrong. It was necessary to make the world go round, and allow people to climb up and down the stairway of life wearing these very same shoes. But there was more to it than that. Though what was it, where was it, and how could it be balanced out?

~~~

Marianne and Albert saw a lot of each other. They ate out together, sometimes they met at work, they spent evenings and weekends together, made love and appeared to enjoy it all. But quite often Albert turned surly, and his behavior became a bothersome black cloud looming over their relationship.

Slowly, and without wanting to, Marianne distanced herself from this undecided and negative man. She, too, was going through what was not exactly a happy phase, and when together they now and then gave the impression that consuming the air they breathed was just another waste of time.

He complained and she looked for a solution.

But instead, the solution found her.

SUNSET IN SARASOTA

CHAPTER 13

Marianne had gone to Europe to participate, along with other colleagues, in a merger between a British company and an Italian company. In reality, an investment bank was buying control of the British firm, and would then take over the Italian one. She traveled back and forth between London and Milan. Short, intense, boring trips—the same routine every time.

But this time something unexpected came up, which grabbed her attention day after day. Among the group was an American from San Francisco who had lived in Europe for more than 10 years. He was based in London, but traveled often. He spoke a little French, got by in German, and, strangely enough, enjoyed conversing in Italian.

"Italy," he always said, "is a country that's truly enjoyable, if you don't take it too seriously. You have to watch out, though, and not get caught up in the system's pitfalls. You've got to measure your visits, as if you were taking a dive into its shimmering blue waters, then a swim and then out."

Marianne knew life in London fairly well. It was the financial capital of Europe, while the UK was America's first cousin. She had been to Italy a few times, enough to note the huge differences between the various regions. She had even wondered if it was really a single nation, or whether Italy was in reality an agglomeration of peoples with the same laws, which each interpreted differently, according to the latitude they lived at. She knew that this was a hurried oversimplification, and realized that an in-depth understanding would take time and commitment. And these were luxuries that she could not afford. She was better off focusing on other, more rational and agile markets.

This time she let her self get carried away, because the operation was big and interesting. It was being conducted by people familiar with European problems, experts at harmonizing financial relations between various countries and continents.

She realized that she was almost having fun, a sensation she hadn't experienced in quite a while.

Maybe it was the great variety of foods and Italian wine, or perhaps the thrills linked to this new project, the people involved and their wide range of personalities. Or maybe it was the guy from San Francisco, half American and half European, who was slowly working his way under her skin—that is, under her dress and over her skin. To get under the skin and reach as far as the soul was a lengthy journey. A doubt arose within her. Hadn't she already reached her spirit, and now, slowly, was going back along the same path, exiting from the skin and stopping under her dress?

He was a real sweetheart, with an awesome sense of humor, and tall enough, though when she wore heels she was as tall as he. He had brown hair, was not overly thin, but well proportioned. His name was Roy.

It seemed to Marianne that it was Roy's smile that set him apart from other men, along with the vivaciousness that sprung from his eyes and his cheerful, pert, solar demeanor—rare qualities in men who worked in this profession. Yet, he was a success. Perhaps it was these characteristics that helped him do business with the Europeans, who usually view American financiers as a bunch of over-serious louts fond of dressing in dark hues—even the women among them. At most, they wore pinstripes. Roy was a bit more freewheeling when it came to dressing, favoring a style somewhere between British and Italian. He had thick hair, and wore it somewhat messy.

After a couple of intense days of work in Milan,

some people in the group decided to spend a weekend at Portofino.

The deal was heading toward conclusion and thoughts of the return trip were already cropping up. At Portofino there was a briskness in the sea air, the food and wine were good, and the view from the Hotel Splendido was enchanting.

That night Roy managed to find his way between Marianne's sheets.

Marianne was not accustomed to letting herself go so quickly and impulsively. She was a woman who thought things out, reasoned so as to prepare her spirit for each small, new step. But without realizing it, for days her spirit had been prepared by Roy.

~~~

Albert became a distant thought, to be associated only with commitments and problems. Lately he had become terribly moody, and the two of them had seen less and less of one another. During this entire trip she had called him twice—two brief superficial calls. He hadn't called her at all. The distance between Marianne and Albert had grown much further than the ocean that lay between them. The thing that most amazed her was that she awoke the next morning feeling gratified. By dawn, Roy was already back in his own room. She had breakfast by herself on the terrace. She breathed in the scent of nature and smiled. She had the feeling that she was no longer alone.

CHAPTER 14

Many American women are attracted to Europe.

At first glance, life there seems to follow a more interior path, there's something more human about it, and as far as Italy is concerned, more romantic. Everything appears simpler, more comprehensible and tolerant.

Unfortunately, tourists are unaware that often, when passing from visitor status to actually becoming a resident, this view is shattered into tiny pieces.

Many do not lose heart, comforted by the fact that they possess an American passport and can return to the States whenever they want. For this reason they don't realize that each day they stoop to new and strange compromises they never would have accepted in their home country—and they've slowly gotten accustomed to them.

But wanting is one thing and deciding is something else. Making decisions means making a break with bonds and the daily routine, cutting yourself off from set plans that involve others. In short, it becomes a kind of re-immigration, a re-inventing of oneself, a distancing from something that is, in the end, harmful no matter how much you may like it.

Marianne had already been living in a mental state that was primed for change. Hers was the kind of active and curious personality that always accompanies intelligence. The idea of making a change seemed irresistible. This time, she made a more radical decision. She quit her job and moved to London, where she picked up a part-time job working for another British-American brokerage house. Now she could reside in Europe. Her new goal was to become a consultant and later on open her own office, where she could work the hours she wanted, with the clients of her choice. Or at least she thought, without yet knowing that working for yourself often meant more commitment and less money. The illusion of being one's own boss, however, always looms great.

All this happened in three months. In that short

time, Albert had barely realized what was going on. It looked like just another of this career woman's experiments, which even she herself was indifferent to. It dawned on him that women, especially the smart ones, are often unpredictable—and that was their allure.

After a while he began to feel her absence. He then felt something more—the distance of her spirit.

They talked on the phone. Albert began calling more frequently, until one day he decided to go to London. As soon as he arrived she told him that she was on her way to Italy. She didn't even attempt to make up an excuse about work. She told him flat out, "I have fun in that country, and I go with a friend I'm very close to. I go fairly often."

When Marianne explained that her friend wasn't in Italy waiting for her, but lived with her in London, and what's more was no exotic lover but an American just like he was, Albert felt useless to himself and to Marianne.

That day they talked for hours.

She was sweet, but it was obvious that she began getting jumpy. Albert had showed up that morning, they ate lunch together and at four in the afternoon were still talking.

"But why weren't you straight with me over the phone?" asked Albert.

"Because I wasn't sure of myself and I didn't want to hurt you. I also figured that you had grown so distant from me. You were acting so weird. I have to confess, there were times when I wondered why

I kept going out with a guy who insisted on not wanting to communicate. Were you afraid that if our relationship had gotten more intense, it would have forced you to totally change your life's goals? You came off as so negative, closed and selfish. I wanted to seek out new horizons, but that was no good for you. I'm convinced that for you I'm just a problem that unsettles and, in the end, saddens you."

Albert fell silent.

He looked at her as if for the first time, now that she was on the verge of leaving him for good.

Before, he had never stopped to think that something like this could happen. It seemed natural to him to meet, talk about work, and discuss a change that in reality would never occur. In short, it was a fun game.

But Marianne kept coming on like a freight train, waxing cruel even, as often infatuated women can be.

"If I had any doubts, they've disappeared completely today. When I look at you, so professional, such a prisoner of logic without any real future apart from high finance; when I look in your eyes all I see is the search for a practical solution, and I ask myself how I ever could have shared my feelings and desires with you for so long. I met a man, or rather, he met me—a man who's glowing and bursting with ideas. It was destiny."

Albert was shocked. He felt immensely alone, though he didn't have the courage to say so.

"You don't understand right now, but we are a

couple. Maybe we were still trying to find one another, maybe I'm a little slow in picking up on your thoughts. I've surely been the way you've described me, now I understand. But let me tell you once again, there's only one thing I'm sure of, and it's that we're a couple.

"You belong to me and I belong to you, and you'll never be able to break this bond.

"I'm sorry for the guy who's gotten between us while you and I were still trying to work things out. He's going to suffer over it one day, if he's really the kind of person you've described him as. He's bound to suffer because he unwittingly found himself between two people who, through pleasure, desperation and rage, remain a couple. This I know for certain. One day you'll figure it out, too, and I'll be there, ready to love you."

He got up and held out his hand, which she shook. She remained seated, baffled, speechless.

He said simply, "Have fun, enjoy life, but remember, we'll get back together. We're a couple. Actually we're *the* couple. Whether you like it or not."

He turned and walked toward the street to hail a cab.

Marianne felt discomfort, as if something were bothering her, but at the same time Albert's parting words struck her with a strange sensation of inevitability.

SUNSET IN SARASOTA

CHAPTER 15

In New York Albert went through the motions of the usual routine, but his passion for work had thoroughly disappeared. He worked only to earn money, only because he had to. It was the rule of the world. He called on all his experience and knowledge of his own kind to keep his lack of desire from showing through. He had not yet acquired the courage to change his life completely and knew that in a world as competitive as this, it would take a serious commitment toward work in order to succeed.

He thought how groundless the rest of the world's perception of the United States was—that all Americans were after, and that all they talked about, was money. This idea must surely have been influenced by areas like New York and southern California, and as a result, all Americans were considered capitalism's ravenous children.

In reality, it was much different.

Capitalism taught how to use money to live each day as best as one could afford, not only to accumulate money or to use it to abuse others.

The egoism of American capitalism is much more subtle: "I want to be happy and have the means, but I want others around me to be happy as well, even if their possibilities are less, otherwise my life would become hell, an ongoing battle to maintain a standard of living and its relative pleasures."

On the other hand, communism, or socialism, has always achieved the opposite while preaching equality. The most extreme example is Russia, both during and after the fall of the communist regime. Power and wealth concentrated in the hands of just a few violent characters.

But what's the use of this sort of reasoning? You simply have to work and make money to live, and that's common throughout the world.

~~~

Albert had but two possibilities: either enjoy himself working or work half-heartedly just to get money to buy his fun. For the first time in his life he had worked out such simple, linear reasoning on how to organize his life. Until then he had lived in a somewhat confused atmosphere, amid commitments, pleasures, fun and relationships. Separating the two worlds was the most commonly used route, but it was also very sad and exhausting. It was like living more than one life at the same time, one of which was slightly alienating.

At any rate, for now he had no other options. He no longer enjoyed work. So he decided to take more vacation time, to travel. He became a guest at friends' homes. He went to the theater more often. He learned to appreciate music.

He began showing up at golf and tennis clubs. He was invited to many parties. He met many people with problems similar to his own, and it was only now, and for the first time in his life, that he realized how many such people there were. The clubs were full of them.

He also discovered that a single, pleasant, financially stable man has excellent chances of stirring the interest of beautiful women. He amazed himself on more than one occasion. He had never realized how easy it was—because he had never dedicated much of his time to an activity as old as mankind itself.

He had met Marianne on the job. At that time he thought it was some great, unexpected stroke of good fortune, practically an opportunity never to be repeated.

So it was true—the world is a many-faceted place, there's room for lots of experiences. Actually, reality goes way beyond the fantasy of stories read in books or seen at the movies.

Once in a while, though, he still called Marianne.
He knew this embarrassed her, but he couldn't resist telling her about his adventures. He also could
not resist trying to guess at and imagine her reactions—the deepest and most secret ones. For her
part, Marianne was reserved and elusive, as often
women can be when it comes to revealing intimate
sensations.

CHAPTER 16

Albert was in Vermont, staying at the home of a lady friend, Jennifer, who he'd been seeing a lot of lately. The house was pleasantly situated upon a large stretch of land. Hills, lakes, fields, trees and meadows in bloom were in view. Although it was July, the air was still fine. Lunch was eaten on the porch, while in the evening it was better to dine inside and leave the windows ajar.

Jennifer was bright and cheery, and full of life. She was a nature-lover and crazy about the mountains. She spent much of the summer at her Vermont cottage, and in the winter she took frequent trips to Colorado, or to the Alps, because she loved to ski. She had been married to a wealthy man, whom she found boring and unbearable. A mistake of youth, perhaps due to the kinds of people their families, both rich, associated with. But Jennifer possessed a free spirit and was hardly ever bogged down with work commitments. She had also written several books—on cooking, tips on finding the best mountain itineraries, and subjects like that. She had a nice income and led a comfortable but by no means extravagant lifestyle.

Her cottage was cozy, full of a thousand little things—wooden objects, birdhouses, old skis, particular stones, some of which were painted, photos of mountain adventures, and so on. She received lots of invitations because she was a fun person, bubbly and pretty. She had a long, thin figure that gave you the idea that it had been hewn from a steel spring. Blond hair, light blue eyes. She looked at people intensely, with a smile always pressed upon her face.

She wasn't a big fan of discussing her past, much less her age. "You're only as old as you feel inside, as old as your spirit communicates to others," she would say. She must have been around forty, though it was hard to say because today's women seem to have come up with the recipe for beating old age. What's more, Jennifer was so athletic and vibrant that at times she looked like a teenager.

A year and a half had gone by since Albert's last meeting with Marianne in London. He had seen her twice in New York after that, in the company of others. They'd barely said anything to one another. He tried to communicate as much as he could, sprinkling his conversation with lots of tiny details that he hoped would spark her curiosity. On the contrary, she seemed to be listening only out of politeness, at the same time trying to free her mind of the insistent presence of the person talking to her and the images he re-evoked. This was the same way he had acted on the phone.

Albert stubbornly repeated to himself that no matter what she said or did, his feelings for her would not change—even if she had been lured away by another man, with whom she surely must have made gratifying love.

When he spoke to her, he perceived her as a creature who was actually a part of his very self. In truth, he did not know what this feeling meant, and what could have led him to a belief that was so deeply rooted in his spirit. For him, it was like having an extra stock of life at his disposal. He felt like the president of the United States, courting the oil-producing countries while all the time knowing that he's already got a huge stock of oil reserves on hand, and other forms of energy as well, and that he'll always find some country ready to sell him oil anyway.

These meetings and phone calls left their mark, deep and permanent, inside him, though he was at a loss to decipher it. One thing for certain, after leaving her or hanging up the phone, he felt enriched with something. It had been like that for many months, but then he began growing closer to Jennifer. With her, everything was much simpler. Never any real problems, just the joy of doing something together and the satisfaction of making love.

Perhaps he was finally getting over the "Marianne virus." With the passing of time, the words uttered in a café in London seemed to fade. When he gave it any thought, it now looked so much like some overacted theatrical exit.

Yet, when he tried to laugh it off, he sensed an implacable sensation whispering to him, "Do not underestimate her. Those words were spoken directly from your heart."

~~~

It was a lovely Sunday night. Jennifer and Albert had taken a long walk that day, through woods and fields. After a little dinner, washed down by a good bottle of red wine, a little small talk, a quick look at the television to check the weather forecast and the latest news, they went to bed.

The bed was big and, considering their tiredness, more comfortable than usual. Albert had taken a couple of days off work to make it a long weekend, four full days to spend with Jennifer. He'd gotten in late Friday night, and it was still only Sunday.

Jennifer read in bed, as Albert drifted off into a peaceful sleep almost immediately. His mind refused to reflect. He didn't have to get back to New York's chaos for another two days. Strange, he once loved the city so, along with his job and all around him. He awoke at about five the next morning.

Outside it was still dark, but the hour on the clock beside the bed was clearly visible. They always left a light on in the house and they slept with the bedroom door open. Neither liked complete darkness. It was nice to open your eyes and recognize objects, and have the sensation that you knew where you were, and be able to exchange glances. Quite reassuring.

Everything was reassuring with Jennifer. He rolled over and looked at her as she slept. Many women, once they take off their make-up, look like someone else. But not Jennifer. She actually looked even younger without it, her face expressed an even more vibrant joy for life. He thought how lucky he was to have met her. He adored her simplicity in interpreting life's events and finding solutions.

He could not resist. He took her in his arms and plied her body with soft kisses.

Unlike Albert, Jennifer slept in the nude. She roused and slowly began moving, returning his caresses. She did not seem at all bothered about having been woken up. She reacted as if this were completely normal. They made love, long and slow, though without great passion. There was an air of vacation and relaxation. When they finished, they found themselves sitting with their backs against the headboard, talking.

Albert still had a lot to learn about life. He was haunted by a funny feeling, but couldn't understand why. He heard Jennifer ask him, "Are you still in love with Marianne?"

"Why do you ask that now, when I feel so good?"

"You're not at peace with yourself, even if you don't want to admit it. Why are you wasting your time with me? Don't get me wrong, I like you a lot, and I feel good being with you. But I've got no one in my life who's that important. At least, I haven't found that person. I love being free, I love nature and the universe, and hope to one day fall head over heels for a man who can dedicate his soul to me. This may never happen, but that's okay just the same. You love Marianne. Inside you, you consider her your woman, but you're not completely aware of this. You cannot grasp the reality of your emotions. Your mind is in a state of rejection and you're confused by your everyday interests. You like me, I don't pose any problems. Why not take advantage of what life has to offer? Carpe diem! It's just that, that woman's roots are sunk so deep within you! Why don't you tell her and get it over with. Marry her!"

Albert looked like a beaten hound. But a twinkling lit up his eyes and he asked her, "How do you know? I've never told you anything in particular about her."

"True. But you do talk about her. And any woman worth her salt understands these things and does not want to hold onto a man just because he's all right by her. You owe me the same clarity of behavior if you want my continued esteem."

"She's in love with someone else, somebody in London. I can't manage to start up any positive communication."

Jennifer took his hand, turned and looked him straight in the eye and said, "Forget about all that! Answer me: did you ask her to marry you?"

He sat there in silence. Then, somewhat ashamed, he replied, "She was the one who asked me to marry her."

"And you, lion heart, answered…?"

"I don't even remember anymore, it was so long ago. But since then I've been blocked. I didn't mention it for quite a while, when she was making her decision to break away from Wall Street and lead a different life."

"You let a career woman like that get away, when she realizes how vain and superficial working on Wall Street is, and you have the courage to look for something new? Don't you have a clue? I had you pegged for someone more intelligent than that…"

Albert bent over her, gave her a kiss, caressed her face and got out of bed. He gathered up his things about the room, went to the bathroom, returned and gathered some more.

"Thanks," he said. "I never thought you were so smart and cunning. Thanks a lot. I'll never forget it. I feel that great esteem and friendship has been born between the two of us."

"Go, run. I'm just sensitive. Intelligence isn't always helpful to a woman, but an open honest heart is. Believe me, happiness is definitely worth looking for!"

She blew him a kiss and rolled over to get back to sleep.

It was still dark.

SUNSET IN SARASOTA

CHAPTER 17

Driving toward home, Albert thought, "Jennifer makes it sound so easy. Now what do I do? If I call her and say, 'Will you marry me?' she'll hang up in my face. If I go to London, she might even refuse to see me.

What have I gotten to thinking? I felt so great up in Vermont…"

While attempting to assess all the difficulties involved, his brain was feverishly at work exploring possible solutions. He suddenly recalled that Marianne's parents still lived in New Jersey. He had gone twice with her to visit them. They were still self-sufficient and appeared to be a lively couple, somewhat resigned to the turbulent life their daughter led and her infrequent visits.

That afternoon he found himself in front of their house.

It had taken him a while to find it, because he'd only vaguely remembered the place. But at last he was there and thought, "What am I doing in front of this house? What do these two people have to do with any of this? They're Marianne's parents, though they don't seem to have much influence over her life. Maybe they don't even know where she is right now."

But by now he was there, all he had to do was get out of the car and go ring the bell. Maybe they weren't home. Why hadn't he called first? He felt he was being intrusive, impolite and perhaps somewhat stupid. Going to their house without even calling first! Still, it was only 2 p.m., not too late.

"What'll I say?"

He decided to make his move. He walked across the front yard and rang the bell. Marianne's father, Thomas, opened the door. He was a pleasant person with thick white hair and an open face. He was fairly tall and still in good shape.

"Sorry to disturb you, I'm...."

"I remember you very well, Albert. Please, come in! What good wind has brought you round these parts? My wife's at a friend's, but she should be back soon. I'm glad to see you." He hesitated and looked hard at Albert. "Has something happened to Marianne! She called last night from London."

"No, no, she's fine, don't worry. I'm here to…"

Thomas looked visibly relieved and his color came back to him. They walked into the living room and sat down. Albert felt a bit more relaxed now; he now knew she was still living in London, and he realized that her father had taken a liking to him.

"I'll get us something to drink. What would you like? White wine, or some water, a Coke or something stronger. A whisky or a martini? I make pretty good martinis. Well…it's a chance for me to have something to drink, too."

"What are you having?"

"Whisky on the rocks, with a splash of water."

"Too strong for me. I'll go with a white wine."

"Great. I'll be right back. I'm really glad to see you, seems like Marianne's here, too."

Albert wondered what her father meant by that, but said nothing to him. The wine and a few pretzels helped him relax a little.

After commenting on the weather, politics, the war in the Middle East, and the economy, Thomas began to reveal some slight embarrassment. He surely could not figure out what Albert had come for, and imagined something strange was going on.

A moment of absolute silence was broken by Albert, who mustered up his courage and said, "I've come for a very specific reason. I know Marianne is super independent, and I have no idea whether she talks to you or your wife about her personal matters. It's just that, I didn't know where to begin, and needed to talk to someone who loves her."

"Of course, of course; you picked the right person. Marianne and I don't see a lot of one another, but we talk often. Actually, I participate a great deal in her decisions and in her life's developments. More than you might think."

"Well, if that's the case then I can skip all the preliminaries and get right to the point. I want to marry Marianne, and I'm here to ask whether you or your wife have anything against it."

Thomas smiled and set his glass down on the coffee table.

"Why, that's great news!" Thomas said with an amused look. "But why ask for my opinion? You know Marianne well enough to know how headstrong and independent she is. I doubt my opinion counts very much when it comes to a decision like this."

When Albert remained silent, Thomas continued.

"Or should I interpret your request as a call for help?"

He stood up and pulled an armchair closer to Albert and sat down facing him. The two men sat for a moment without speaking.

"I really would like to help you, but the mere thought that I might talk about anything of the sort with Marianne makes me laugh," said Thomas.

"I have no problem with your desire to marry my daughter but surely you know that Marianne's engaged and talking about getting married soon. Her fiancé has already bought a new home for them in London."

Thomas leaned closer to Albert and lowered his voice. "Personally, I'm sorry about it. I've met the guy and he's not my type. I really prefer her to be in the United States--closer to us. I've always had a great deal of esteem for you and I never understood why you didn't get married years ago. I think Marianne wanted to. It might be too late now."

Albert smiled and rose from the sofa. He held his hand out to Thomas. "Thomas, your words have given me strength. Winning your daughter back is my job alone. I sought comfort and moral support and you gave me that. And I'll tell you this: there's a plane to London later this afternoon. I should be able to make it; I've already booked a seat."

"Albert, don't rush things. You worry me. I don't want anyone to suffer over this. And by anyone, I especially mean Marianne, but you, too."

Albert was already out the door and running toward his car.

SUNSET IN SARASOTA

CHAPTER 18

Albert had revisited the most important moments of his life many times. He had relived them as if the adventure was repeating itself, but this was the first time he had told them to anyone.

Joy listened with great intensity. These memories had always been tucked away inside him, migrating from brain to heart, from stomach to sex and down the legs, which sometimes shook. Then they turned around and flowed back the way they came.

At last he had shared his story with someone. By chance he had found the strength to share it with a person whose spirit appeared warm and welcoming. She just seemed to have shown up along the way. He surely needed her, but in all honesty, had not been looking for her.

Joy gathered up her own strength to ask him, "What happened after you talked to her father and your trip to London?"

"I swear, I don't exactly remember all the details that led to Marianne changing her mind and marrying me. I don't remember because it all seemed so natural. I knew it would happen that way. I had always been of the conviction that we were a couple, and the other guy was just an interloper who had never understood the strange bond between us. I was sorry for him; he was a nice guy, he was all right. He just never figured out what he'd gotten into.

"I seemed to sense, whether she was making me believe it or whether it was actually true, that Marianne liked the other guy better than me in bed. It got to the point where I said to her, 'Keep him on as a lover. You can see him now and then, if this is what gives you satisfaction. I don't think this will bother our relationship in the slightest, as deep as it is, beyond the details set forth by our social system. After all, the search for personal joy and pleasure is not a sin, if no one is hurt by it.'

"Today I wonder whether, with the passing of time, a situation like that would have worked. But there was no need for it. After four months of pushing and shoving, Marianne disappeared for a month, to a destination that only her family knew and kept secret. She returned and two months later we got married. How things ever completely turned around like that I still don't know. But the explanation for this is simple: we really were a couple—born to grow or sink together."

Joy, the romantic, was shocked and very excited by all of this.

It was a beautiful story, simple and deep. She went so far as to put Marianne's disappearance into the background, behind the values of the universe that had conspired to create this adventure. That was Joy, or so at least she seemed.

Each of us can make up his or her own mind.

"What ever happened to Roy?" she asked.

"No great shakes. Kept working, got married, went back to San Francisco. Now he's married to a young South American woman. All three of us have seen each other more than once, actually, all four of us, since his first wife was with him. We're still friends. I think everybody's got it worked out for themselves."

Marianne was, I mean, is, a woman who knows how to create an atmosphere of serene respect which makes everyone feel comfortable."

"What do you mean, is?"

"Well, I don't know where she is. I just know that she exists."

SUNSET IN SARASOTA

CHAPTER 19

Even in the past when they had spent much time at their house in Siesta Key, Marianne and Albert maintained their official residence in New York. Thus, in the long list of 9-11 victims her name went unnoticed in Sarasota. When Albert sold that house, the neighbors figured the two had decided to return to New York. The two still hadn't had any solid local friendships. No one really knew whether they were married for a long time or even married at all.

The house itself was rife with memories. Albert bought an apartment downtown. He reappeared on the scene three months later, though he began associating with a whole different crowd. Without Marianne behind him, he took up the role of the semi-retired Wall Street type who'd been out of work for a while. He began hitting the country clubs, which were a natural meeting point for people with this kind of experience.

In reality, he was re-starting from zero upon the path that would lead to self-understanding.

He now carried within him a new experience with which he hadn't the foggiest idea how to live. Marianne was somewhere else. After a heap of indecision, plans and love stories, Marianne really was somewhere else. But Albert still could not comprehend this. He now went to his tiny office nearly every day. He had a secretary who was also taking care of company accounting, and a supervisor who earned a commission on sales in addition to his regular salary. He rented these three rooms from his architect friend and partner, who followed construction and occupied the rest of the floor with his own office. It was a good set-up, in that it allowed Albert to avoid a full-time commitment while giving him the freedom to explore lots of different things.

He had begun being active in the art world. Out of politeness and unaware of the intensity of their relationship, no one asked him about Marianne. He never mentioned her; he didn't know what to say.

They weren't divorced and as far as he was concerned, she wasn't dead. Her body had never been found. For him, Marianne was simply somewhere else. It seemed to him that he knew for sure. But where? When he dreamed of Marianne, she appeared so real that he'd walk around happy for days. Marianne was all right, smiling all the time, having found the solution to all her problems.

Where was she?

Could they ever get back together to be the couple he had always considered was destined to be?

Failing to come up with an explanation for any of it, Albert decided that from then on he'd live life just to live, without asking himself too many questions. Wasn't that what we were made for?

He had read a book of poetry that began like this:

You live
because life of
life is born
and no one knows
where the border of death lies.
Death may border on
a new life
and you must live to find out.

He decided to live by this motto. He wrote it in large letters on a sheet of paper and framed it, then hung it in plain view in his office.

Then he met Joy.

SUNSET IN SARASOTA

CHAPTER 20

The new project was moving along fairly well. Albert was excited about watching the buildings rise up from the ground. This was the first time he himself had actually ever participated in something concrete, basing his work on his own skills and know-how. And since it was the first time in this type of project, he had made many decisions somewhat lightly, and profits, in fact, would be quite low. He also had tangible, nagging competition on his back. He could not order a director to cut costs, improve marketing and raise prices. He was the director, and at times, looking around, he felt a little lost, alarmed even. At any rate, considering the solid state of his finances and the relatively small financial commitment being made on this project, it didn't much matter whether profits were high or not. In truth, the project was there to keep him busy, something to keep his attention focused on very positive and real things. He had embarked upon a new way of living and solving problems.

More than once he thought what a thrill it must be to design an airplane or to direct a film, to participate in the adventure of building a space shuttle, to compose a successful symphony or even simply to conceive, like a father, of an object that people adopt as part of their existence.

"To be a father." He hadn't had time to experience that thrill with Marianne. If it had been otherwise, now he would have a person who acted and thought, someone with whom he could communicate and evolve. A creature who, through thick and thin, would attract Albert's attention to the point of wiping out the emptiness he carried deep inside him.

Albert realized that the whirlwind of activity that had consumed him until a few years ago, had been useless.

Marianne had understood this before he had, and initiated him into things that were more real than the ones generated by the hodgepodge of predators great and small that frequent the stock exchange and have no vision other than moving paper to make money.

He remembered how a news item could make the market lag, while two days later business would be booming again as if whatever had been such important news were deleted in its entirety. But that news was still there, two days hadn't changed anything. It's just that the market had "digested" it and it was now necessary to resort to some other stratagem to move shares, earn commissions, make profits out of sales.

The five-year plans of companies, the solid foundations of many businesses, were of no importance. What counted were earnings over the three-month period, which would be more or less adjusted depending on whether you wanted the price of a given share to rise or fall.

How different America had been in the days of the founders of Ford, General Electric, Boeing, and so forth. Those people needed capital for long-term plans, to run real factories with long-term balanced budgets and huge growth forecasts, where immediate earnings were often not the topmost priority.

What had happened? Buy, sell, buy, sell, mergers, buy-outs, etc...

Then everyone's eyes are focused on that little group on the stage at the New York Stock Exchange on Wall Street, applauding and smiling brightly, thinking only one thing: Whatever happens, I've made some money.

The incredible thing is that these people are convinced they've earned their money through hard work.

But why had it taken Marianne to get him to understand and why had he taken so long to accept it, thereby hindering the evolution of her mood as well? They had wasted too much time in making a decision, in chasing one another around, in an attempt at seeking out their own spirits and reorganizing them.

They had been too afraid to burn their bridges and break away from the lifestyle that had taught them how to make easy money.

Perhaps a hidden fear of dedicating themselves to something new and unknown also put a wrench in their decision-making. They saw problems in the lives of others, their real apprehensions, and felt as if they were outsiders compared to all that struggling. The work they were accustomed to gave them the faculty of criticizing, advising, adjusting statements, always above and beyond everyday considerations and problems.

They had thought of changing careers, but they always returned to the original program—slowly detach themselves from the system, take time out to enjoy life, try to get by on less income while working less, but taking advantage of friends and experience accumulated in the business. As it so happened, they had tucked away a decent amount of savings, allowing them to take their time in making a decision.

This lack of determination was the worst mistake of their lives, and brought Marianne to the World Trade Center Twin Towers that fateful September morning.

~~~

Back then Marianne and Albert spent much time at a house on Siesta Key, an island just a few minutes' drive from downtown Sarasota. It was a new experience.

They had a nice yard, small but with a very tropical pool. The property lay on the shores of a canal, where Albert kept a motorboat. Sometimes they went to New York, where they still had an apartment, to maintain their work connections. True, most of the work could have been done online or over the phone, but physical encounters do have their importance.

Inside, they felt that this type of lifestyle was somewhat false. They were hovering at midstream and maybe it would always be that way. They enjoyed gardening, reading and art, which, in Sarasota, was flourishing. They did, however, realize they were not actual gardeners or artists or writers. They found themselves caught up by the allure of Florida life, slowly becoming enchanted with the slower pace and calmer existence. They hailed from a fast-paced world where people were valued not necessarily by their actions—but by their connections to an elite group of movers and shakers in the business arena. In reality, their job was to provide hard-copy support, which miraculously brought capital to those who knew how to apply an idea to a concrete project, which, in turn, generated work and multiplied the investment—at least on paper.

Whatever happened afterward, with the passing of time, was part of another film.

In any case, they were slowly approaching the other side of the river: reality. They were considering several different possibilities and discussed them with friends.

It was a very intense week for Marianne. She gave up all her usual Sarasota pastimes and glued herself to the computer and the telephone. She had stumbled upon a deal that would earn her a nice chunk of cash. It was a good idea not to pass up such an opportunity. Afterward they would take a nice trip and have more capital to set out on another, different adventure.

~~~

One evening she said to Albert, "I've got to go to New York for five days. Unfortunately, I have to meet these people at their offices in the World Trade Center."

She flew to New York on September 8, 2001.

CHAPTER 21

The disc of the sun was red, perfectly round, sharply defined and large. It steadily made its downward course toward the ocean's surface. It moved quickly, giving life to one of those famous west coast Florida sunsets.

Lido Beach and the road along it were crowded with people posed practically in adoration, with attentive looks in their eyes and intense facial expressions. Who knows how each one of them utilized that moment to nourish his or her own thoughts? Some held cameras, or even had them mounted on tripods.

This scene repeated itself punctually every evening that the sky was clear and promised a beautiful sunset. The odd thing was, not all of the people gathered there were tourists. Many were local regulars who recognized one another.

What was it that this repeated, forceful phenomenon said to them?

Albert had first heard about the Sarasota sunset in New York from enthusiastic friends. He hadn't really given it much thought, though. He had traveled widely, had seen a thousand sunsets and figured that the sun was, after all, always the same.

Albert was sitting on a little wall along the beach, next to Joy, concentrating on the sun going down. It seemed to melt like ice cream does when it touches a warm surface, in this case the sea.

This, of course, was the exact opposite of the way it was in reality. The sun was incandescent, but distant, while the waters of the ocean could not even hope to put it out—if the sun could be immersed in the ocean, the water would be vaporized and dispersed—who knows where—in a flash. For an instant we'd be blown by a great wind and be able to see the land that had been covered up by the sea. Then it would all come to an end.

For now, though, the system went on functioning punctually. The base of the red circle widened, its shape now neither well-defined nor round. Streaks of slightly different tones of red could soon be seen. The sea swallowed up the sun, the atmosphere enveloped it.

What a grand illusion!

Then the last orange hump lingered an instant before disappearing. The colors were diffused through the sky and over the sea, buildings, beaches, trees and clouds, which all suddenly seemed to change lives.

Sarasota was covered by that almost yellow and unique light described so well by the writer John McDonald. Albert had read a few of his books and thought at first that McDonald's description of this mystical light was just poetic dribble. Now he lived immersed in that very same light.

Once the show is over people begin to move, and someone asks you if you saw the green flash. There are loads of stories on this phenomenon, but the most interesting thing is that some people swear they've actually seen it. Others are not so sure, while others say they definitely have not seen it.

Albert was one of those who were not completely sure. Two or three times he thought he almost spotted it, but it happened so fast that he wondered whether it had been real or whether his imagination had tricked him to make him happy.

He took Joy by the hand and like two school kids they walked toward the car parked five hundred yards down the beach. At Albert's place they made themselves a nice little dinner, and then went for an ice cream at Jolly's, the nearby ice cream parlor.

They did not talk much, but felt at peace with themselves.

They decided to sleep together and made love

with such tenderness that they forgot all about why they were together and what it was they wanted from the future. It was Saturday and the next day they could roll around in bed until late, have breakfast, read and fill their spirits with a little R & R.

CHAPTER 22

The next morning they woke up early. Indeed, the night before they had left the curtains open on purpose so they could fall asleep with the starry sky in their eyes. At sunrise, the light began working its way into their dreams – softly at first, as the window faced west. They awoke, dozed off again, but by eight a.m. they decided they'd had enough of staying in bed. They got up feeling full of strength and desire to live.

They read for a while, hugged, drank tea, roamed around the apartment, listened to music, talked, looked out at the distant sea, gazed up at the sky.

They talked some more and then looked at one another as if to ask:

"We're bursting with desire to live, what shall we do today?"

They decided to go to the Colony, a resort-tennis club on Longboat Key beach, just few minutes' drive by car. The club served an excellent Sunday brunch. Then they would take it from there.

On second thought, they rode their bikes instead of using the car, taking advantage of the opportunity for a little exercise and enjoying the fine weather. Brunch supplied them with a burst of energy, though it wasn't as if they were in need. After that, they rented a catamaran on the beach and, as they say, they took to the open sea.

Though Albert owned a motorboat for convenience, he had always loved to do a little sailing. He was originally from Rhode Island, which indeed could boast great sailing traditions, even if those traditions seem to have been forgotten lately. He was not an expert, but he knew how to handle a sailboat, and had been a guest on many.

That small, light and fast catamaran filled them with delight, gliding upon the turquoise sea as if across a giant sheet of ice. They stayed out for a long time, and at one point even considered waiting to see the sunset before heading back to the beach. But sunset was still hours away and for now the sun's intensity still had to be reckoned with. So they headed back to shore and returned to Albert's house by bike.

They were tired but as happy as school kids playing hooky. Without saying so, both felt certain that the memory of that day would dwell within their spirits for a long time to come. They also wondered, in silence, whether a lasting and satisfying relationship for both could ever rise up out of the ashes of the past. It may have been a bit rash or premature to go asking such questions, and for the moment neither of them dared utter anything of the sort.

They sat in the den with the TV on, though they were not really watching it.

Then Joy broke the silence. "Albert, I really had a great time today. It's so much fun doing things with you. You're down to earth; you live for today. I wonder what you used to be like, when you worked on Wall Street. I can't imagine you there at all.

"With Greg, everything was so planned out; life was cold, organized down to the smallest detail, void of emotions. Today we rode our bikes, and then went out on the little catamaran—for Greg all that would have been impossible. He always had to ride around in his Mercedes, because like many realtors he thought it gave him status and importance, as if two hundred dollars' more a month in leasing were enough to demonstrate the existence of an enviable financial situation. If you think about it, it's pathetic.

"Everything in his life reflected this mentality—the way he dressed and talked, the people he hung out with, the places he went, the people he wanted to be seen by, the people he made a show of greeting, and all that. If he got on a boat, it could only be an important boat. He hadn't ever wondered why some little boats actually cost more than big ones. Quality, details, performance—those ideas were completely foreign to him. As far as cars went, Mercedes was tops for him. No matter, of course, that in Europe they were used as taxis.

"Oh, he loved to talk about Europe, but actually going there was another story. It would have been a sacrifice, because people there had a different way of living, and he was too lazy to adapt to their lifestyle, even if only for a short time."

"Joy, variety is the spice of life. Don't criticize it. For him, certain things are important. Some of those things may have been important to me, too. Today I see the world somewhat differently, but I won't disavow my past or anyone else who happens to believe in something different. Like that poet I told you about said,

> *You live*
> *because life of*
> *life is born*
> *and no one knows*
> *where the border of death lies*
> *Death may border upon*
> *a new life*
> *and you must live to find out.*

"What do you mean to say?" Joy looked annoyed. "Now you're trying to justify Greg's behavior and defend that whole superficial world that's concerned only with business, interests and politics.

"Weren't you trying to get away from that kind of lifestyle? And what about Marianne, who never had time to fully explain it to you? Maybe she herself hadn't succeeded in completely breaking away, since she eventually died at Ground Zero."

"Marianne's not dead, and I never said she was. Who ever gave you a confirmation on that? Maybe she's somewhere still trying to figure out life. She refused to accept these black-and-white solutions that seem so clear to you. You're ready to exclude from the world anybody who doesn't follow your beliefs."

~~~

Joy felt somewhat ill at ease. She realized she had said too much, especially in pronouncing the word which, in Albert's mind, was still mysterious and off-limits, as far as Marianne was concerned: death. In reality, Marianne was alive, more alive than ever.

She sat for a moment in silence, unsure whether or not to move closer and reassure him. She was a tender woman only in appearance, for underneath she was stubborn and sure of her own opinion.

She stared at him in defiance and said, "If you want, I can go home right now. Then you can drown yourself in your life, and I can do the same in mine. What do you say?"

Albert turned and examined her with intensity, while at the same time forcing himself to keep a certain distance.

"I don't understand you," he replied. "Did you just get stung by a wasp or something? You're free to do whatever you feel.

"That's what's so nice about friendship. We're not married, and it's better that way, because all too often marriage destroys the most basic rules of friendship. That's why I was against marrying Marianne. I had to do it because that's what the system demanded of me, and with the aim of rendering our lives together easier. But what good did it do? It was useless, because whether married or not married, friends or not friends, she would have had to leave. And if she had stayed, I would have forgotten that officially she was my wife.

"She was more than that, she was my soulmate. We were a couple, with or without papers. And that's what I find so ridiculous about gay marriage. They've already got the opportunity to be together without getting sucked up into the black hole of bureaucracy. What is it they're looking for? Legal protection? Let them start up a partnership with terms agreeable to both. Then they may cancel or change the pacts as they wish, without having to go to a judge who reads a report written up by other people and tells you what to do.

"Humanity seeks freedom, but people adore the rules that enchain them."

"I don't want to marry you, so we're in agreement there," said Joy stopping him. "I think we can spend some wonderful time together. The thing is, we have to break away from the mass of the world that doesn't want to understand."

"Understand what?" Albert looked irritated.

"Your theories, their theories, the rules of countries, religions, or the ones called upon in the name of clairvoyance, spiritualism, ecology and so on, tend to forget that we are creatures built to reproduce, argue, live, love, destroy, construct, eat, exercise power, go to the toilet, and are destined to decompose in a blend of dust and worms."

Albert's face became very serious, reminding Joy of a television preacher's expression. He continued, "I really think we're courageous, because we know all this and yet we keep chasing visions much bigger than ourselves, ready to start up again with the complaints and criticism, but in any case set on starting up again. Doesn't this lead you to imagine that we know too little to be sure of all the answers? I believe that one day we will know all the answers, but don't ask me when. Now I have to live and I feel as if I am under siege by a world built on rules, rules, rules. But these rules no longer apply to reality that's been constructed by man- and womankind.

"You see how politically correct, or rather, deviant, I myself am? I say 'man and womankind.'

"Until not very long ago, in a context of this sort, the word 'man' in 'mankind' stood for 'humankind.' But now women are offended by this, as if they were different creatures altogether. In reality, they are—fortunately—different, because it is only thus that we can continue this complex and variegated dance together, where sex is but a single detail to guarantee the procreation of the species, while other differences guarantee much more—which is to say, the quality of the species. The next step will be to specify *Black* mankind, *Black* womankind. *Asian* mankind, *Asian* womankind. *White* mankind, *White* womankind. *Hispanic* mankind, *Hispanic* womankind. And so on down the line with all the others, in order not to offend anybody.

"In reality, it's the most effective way to offend everybody and break the world down into colors that don't mean a thing. The world is already divided up according to aptitudes, religions, intelligence quotients, cultures, skills, tastes, passions, aspirations, and so forth. And this is a boon, otherwise imagine how boring life would be! I think it would be better to recognize these differences right off the bat and use them to improve the system.

"They'll always exist, as there will always be differences in economies and ideals, in attempts to influence life's system and to condition individual freedoms."

Albert paused for an instant as he arived at a conclusion. When he began to speak again it was in a gentle tone.

"Freedom is a difficult word to interpret and explain. It would be necessary to begin from the principle that 'freedom' is more of a duty than a right. This is something that the world today, drunk on this word, tends to forget. In reality, however, this was to be expected, because you can't speed up certain types of evolution. The so-called cultural revolutions, which eventually break into all-out wars, lead only to temporary dominion. Things get back to normal in a short time thereafter. We progress, but we defend the culture and the lifestyle that were fought so hard for."

Only now had Joy begun to understand what kind of chain reaction she had provoked. It was also fueled by the Scotch that Albert kept pouring himself freely, even though he was generally not a big drinker.

Joy suddenly jumped up and interrupted Albert's tedious discourse.

"Would you please put a sock in it and chill?

"No, I wasn't stung by a wasp.

"I just said that because your reply reminded me of the way Greg used to act. He would never take a clear stand on people or events around him. He was non-committal...and this drove me crazy. How can you not detest certain situations or people and not try to change the world when it spins off course?"

"Good question, but here's my previous concept again. Who decides when the world is spinning off course? This question is more difficult to answer than yours."

"Great answer. But what does answering a question with a question mean? In my little circle of friends we always explain our reasoning behind what we say and do. We discuss things for hours, we cite all kinds of websites, books and articles. We always find something gratifying. It's as if you're acting this way on purpose tonight just to get me ticked. You even bring up gay rights and think you can solve the problem with a simplistic flick of the wrist. None of this stuff makes any sense. I think it's better if I go back home."

As she uttered this last phrase, Joy sat down on the couch—uncertain and tired.

Albert got up from his chair and sat down beside her. He held back for a moment, but then caressed her cheek. He did not smile.

His thoughts came through his lips in firmly spoken words. He spoke with determination as if he were trying to prove his point before a large crowd or in a university lecture hall.

"You're right, but still, life is nothing but one big mess. People get off on doubting everything. The more you go looking for a sure answer to everything, the more new rules there are. The more we demand an easy solution generated outside ourselves, and the more we give power to committees and government, the more individuals of all colors and customs lose their very reasons for existing as individuals. Very sad."

"Nice words," Joy commented, "but your ideas seem a little too conservative for me, and fail to protect those who really suffer."

"There will always be those who suffer," said Albert, "that's the way life has been designed. Let's not deceive ourselves so that we end up suffering even more, and get angry to boot, because we feel abandoned unto ourselves—some more, some less. There's just one basic rule to follow and it's this: The more fortunate ones must help the others, which, after all, is in their own best interests as well.

"You can't live a comfortable life with serenity if you're surrounded by sick, starving people willing to do anything just to survive.

"Capitalism's egoism works when left alone, without the use of repression and demagogy.

"Why do you call such a point of view conservative?

"I consider it futuristic, positive and reality-based. I also think it's a way to safeguard 'freedom.' It seems to me that many so-called 'liberal' debates on culture share only the root of the word 'liberty' with the true joy of living and freedom. On the contrary, their acute pessimism drives them to constantly redefine the different classes of individuals. The result is new miseries on top of existing ones, defeating the concept of freedom. These are merely political labels good for TV.

"Please, Joy, try not to be influenced by theories that conceal such interests beneath various strategies. Conservative or liberal, where's the difference? The difference is only in the people."

"Maybe you're right. As for me, I've had enough of this mood of yours and your senseless babbling. I'm going home. Tomorrow morning I have an early appointment with my shrink and I want to get a good night's sleep. Come to think of it, seeing a psychologist would do you good. I find it amazing that in the third millennium there are still people who aren't in analysis, or refuse even to attend those seminars that are so incredibly helpful. I really think it would do you a world of good."

They quickly brushed one another's cheek with a kiss and Albert closed the door behind Joy.

SUNSET IN SARASOTA

CHAPTER 23

The Italian restaurant where Albert often went to eat was bustling. The name "Mediterraneo" brought to mind some very pleasant trips he and Marianne had taken along the shores of that sea of limited dimensions, which, despite its docile appearance, could be capricious and of a changing character.

The Mediterranean Sea's nature may indeed have influenced the history of the peoples who had once lived on its shores and who had basically laid the foundations of western civilization. This constant search for ourselves and our readiness to change directions and experience hail from recollections of the Mediterranean's behavior—now calm, an instant later stormy, and in a few hours azure, soft and caressed by a fragile breeze. Our search is the same as theirs—to have a well organized life that aspires to the "Pax Romana," a dream sent forth beyond one's own national boundaries.

After all, isn't the goal of the Americans similar to the achievements of the ancient Romans?

Such thoughts ran through Albert's mind, so foreign to the place in which he happened to be sitting at a table waiting for Jeff, his architect partner. They were friends and had made plans to meet for dinner.

Three months had passed since that unsettling weekend spent doing all those things with Joy—watching the sunset, riding bikes, renting the catamaran, and especially that absurd argument that had shaken Albert from a sort of hibernation. For some reason he still couldn't quite get a handle on, he wasn't very keen on trying to explain why their relationship, so spontaneous and serene, had all of a sudden changed direction.

Albert began reconsidering Greg and could now better understand the reasons behind his behavior.

That old fight they had once had at the restaurant had looked so much different to Albert back then. Greg was not as cold and superficial as the events of that evening and various comments here and there had made him out to be. Perhaps he was too practical, too attached to making the kind of money that gave him a comfortable life; he was careful about who he socialized with and was somewhat superficial. But once you got to know him it was clear that he was a good person with modest ambitions who believed in the adage "live and let live." Depending on the context of the situation, he may be accused of being indifferent, and for Joy, indifference is a mortal sin.

Albert had begun seeing him again for work and was certain that behind his reaction on that most memorable evening at the restaurant there had been layers and layers of accumulated frustration within Greg that slowly but inexorably brought him to the point of losing control of his good manners. This, of course, was just a theory, a sensation which seemed ever more likely to correspond with the way things really were, in light of the experience Albert had been sharing with Joy.

All this, however, existed practically in a subconscious form, though it would play an increasingly important role in determining Albert's mood.

Jeff walked in as chipper as could be. He had just received a much-desired building permit from the county.

"Got the permit! But no shop talk tonight. Tonight we eat and drink and talk about all kinds of things. Tonight we check out and get checked out."

Albert agreed with enthusiasm. That nonsense about the system bored him to death. After their first glass of wine the topic of conversation slid around to Joy and why she was not with Albert.

"You two have been seeing less and less of each other lately," observed Jeff. "What's up? Some other beauty caught your eye?"

"No. But I don't know what to say, actually. I still see a lot of Joy, though sometimes I feel quite relieved when she goes back to her place. But then I end up missing her, and I ask myself whether it's just a question of sex or mental laziness. When a relationship becomes a habit it's hard to assess it and it's hard to break out of it and seek out another one, especially if you're not so young any more and depend more and more on the cadence of your life."

"But why all the fuss? She seems to be the cheerful type, a live wire, and very concerned about you—besides the fact that she's got a pretty face, a swell pair of legs and hot tits. Those are all qualities that should not go underestimated."

"You're right. It's just that sometimes she bores me so, she tears my personality to shreds."

"Aren't you letting your imagination get the best of you?"

"I'm telling you, I still haven't figured this whole thing out, but it's like...she argues about everything and keeps trying to give you lessons about everything. She reads all those books on seeking universal strength or whatever you call it. She meets with these groups that go on and on about how we should modify our behavior and thought in order to understand, in order to find an answer. What's funny, is they actually find that answer, and think that other people haven't reached their level. You see, she belongs to a category of those in the know. I'm still in a phase with the ones who are trying to ask the right questions."

"You've gotten yourself in a tricky situation. Maybe you're making this out to be...."

"Don't you tell me that I need to see a shrink, too. Joy reminds me every time I see her. She goes twice a week and says anyone who doesn't is boorish and backward, a caveman from the Stone Age."

"I don't think we've ever gotten beyond the Stone Age, man. Just because we've discovered steel, uranium and computers doesn't change anything. We're still fighting over the same problem as our predecessors."

Jeff said this last sentence with such vehemence that it baffled Albert.

"Oh, come on. Let's perk things up a little here. Going for a boat ride this weekend?"

SUNSET IN SARASOTA

CHAPTER 24

A little boat ride, no. But a fierce argument with Joy, yes. The whole thing was over in a flash, like lightning in clear skies.

Indeed, they could no longer even remember why they were fighting. What was the remark, or rather clash of concepts which were most likely foreign to their experience and derived from outside influences that had caused them to react so negatively? But just as these outside influences had worked their way into their relationship, from that day on they would be forgotten. Relaxed from their fatigue, they made love and slept like babies.

In that moment they were surely themselves, isolated from the world and poised to feel united. Outside advice—castles in the air made of fleeting theories that dwell within each of us, which we are actually quite familiar with, and which some people wish to convince us are some kind of new reality that's been verified by them with all the certainty in the world—had hightailed it into the darkness of night.

~~~

That Sunday morning's sun brought with it new strength and reawakened in Joy new visions, filling her with new certainties. Of course, certainties are short-lived in this world, though they may be obstinate and bear great changes we will one day come to regret. This goes for individuals as it does for committees, political parties, nations, and the world as a whole. Indeed, such moments are crucial to the existence of each one of us.

~~~

Albert's right leg had been bothering him for a few days. It hindered his walking and even ached when he was lying in bed. That morning he had the foolish idea to say, "This is the first time in my life I've had trouble walking. What a rotten feeling. I never thought I'd wind up feeling like this at my age, and I'm not that old."

Joy sniffed. "To begin with, you've got to read books by Louise Hay. That way you'll start to understand the reasons. Then you can read other authors; I'll lend you the books, who'll explain why this thing has singled you out. There's surely a message in all this which you must assimilate if you want to change your life."

"Joy," interrupted Albert, "you must certainly be right, but all I want to know now is what's caused this pain and how to get rid of it. Tomorrow I'll go to the doctor. I really hadn't given it much thought until yesterday."

Joy replied with the brashness of an expert addressing a poor illiterate chump.

"You still believe that illnesses and disabilities are generated only by bacteria, viruses, accidents or any other mechanism that a doctor tries to explain to you?"

"Unfortunately, there are many cases that doctors can't explain. But there's definitely a reason, or as you would say, a mechanism behind everything that exists."

"How many times do I have to tell you? Elevate yourself! Everything's up to you and the Universal Force you can—oh, how should I say it?—harmonize with and get hold of… I don't know how else I can make you understand…"

"I understand. I believe in the Universal Force. I believe that we are destined for more important things. I believe in something you can call God, or whatever you want to call it. The problem here is just that my leg hurts and maybe two or three aspirins will help ease the pain. Why should we have to bring in all these big names and theories and…?"

"But you yourself said that you never expected to experience anything like this at your age. What did you mean by that? What sensation was going through your mind? You already saw yourself as old, walking with a cane, or worse yet, riding in an electric wheelchair. You have to understand that if this is what you think, then there's no way out of it—you're already there."

"A lot of what you're saying is right. How we think we are is important, because it surely has an impact on our behavior and our bodies. But I did not want to say that I don't feel young. I don't know why I said what I said, actually. I have a few friends that have had operations on their meniscus. Maybe I was thinking that since I had never had any minor symptoms before this, I didn't expect that the pain in my knee and thigh would come so suddenly. It's a mechanical thing, Joy. That's what the doctor will tell me tomorrow. Could even be sciatica. So please, don't mix the universe with sciatica." He paused.

"Come on, that's enough. Let's go out and have a good breakfast."

Albert's efforts to spend a nice, relaxing Sunday in peace, and enjoy a little boat ride, were in vain.

Joy had to redeem this poor, simple mortal and make him reason. She had to bring him into her world, send him to a psychologist, get him to take courses, introduce him to her group—this would provide Albert with the therapeutic help he needed, as well as a clear explanation which would enable him to overcome his limits.

Albert remembered Gregs's profound rage that evening when the dam of his frustrations burst. He brought Joy home and told her he had to see Jeff.

SUNSET IN SARASOTA

CHAPTER 25

After driving Joy home, Albert went back to his apartment to listen to a little music on his terrace and read.

It was a clear day with a cool breeze blowing from north, northwest. It suddenly dawned on him why he had been so into Marianne. Despite her very strong and unyielding personality, she always sought out the right questions to ask herself, and it was thanks to this self-doubting process she evolved slowly but with profound respect for the people and things that surrounded her.

Unfortunately, humanity generally believes that

the findings of scientists and scholars in general are precise judgments. Science says so. Wholly ignored are the doubts that assail researchers if they're honest. Every scientific discovery starts with a postulate, a statement, an act of faith. This is then elaborated on—and it is only at this point that rationality intervenes. It is no coincidence that mathematical analysis may be defined as a "poetic science," where at times imagination has the upper hand over reality. Without mathematical analysis we'd still be making superficial observations of phenomena, and unable to interpret or extrapolate them.

The concept is easy to grasp—just read one of the many books written on Einstein. This problem is, however, that people do not wish to admit this. Everybody's either looking for a sure explanation for everything or giving you one, non-stop.

You can't explain everything, you have to submit to it. All you can do is interpret it and try to live together in a more constructive way.

~~~

He felt the boredom of Joy rising up in him. How mistaken he'd been. He had her pegged for a chipper lady who drew gratification from her painting and friendships. But he had been way off the mark.

For Joy, painting was an excuse to feel creative and sell a few paintings, which helped top off her already adequate income provided by her inheritance and, to a lesser degree, the alimony her first husband still paid her. Her economic freedom and the lack of true creative drive or personal commitment led to a life whose focus was itself—her own desires and ailments, her victories and losses. And she was not even what one would call success-oriented. She was happy with the certain respect and affection she received from a restricted circle of friends. Whether this respect and affection were true or false, it didn't matter. She basked in the consideration of others and had no intention of going beyond social relations, no matter how deep or long-term.

"Maybe she was right," Albert said to himself. "But why has this woman, who was so bubbly and buoyant at first, become such a burden? Why did she go around preaching other people's theories and then all too often act in complete contrast with those very same theories?"

In the beginning she had given the impression of being very open, but as time went on she became contorted. She always complained about every little thing, especially her physical ailments, which were nothing outrageous, quite normal.

She could turn a toothache into an epic tale, keeping all of her friends up to date on every tiny detail. The doctor, or rather doctors, were bombarded with questions. Albert had to pay close attention to what she said otherwise it would have been interpreted as a great lack of sensitivity toward the "patient." Where had Louise Hay's books gone?

~~~

Albert took up pen and paper to write a few lines, which he would enclose in an envelope and slip inside his building's mailbox on his way out. He knew he would spend such a gorgeous afternoon out somewhere, but doing what?

Those few lines, which were addressed to Joy, went simply:

You belong to the category of people who know.

I'm adrift upon my ignorance, which is still at a stage where I'm seeking the right questions and how to ask them. The answers are so far off that I can't even dare to imagine them.

Sometimes I think I can make out a question that seems logical, and I begin to entertain a certain timid relationship with what I believe might be an adequate answer. Usually this is a pretty quick turn of events, because I wind up getting confused and changing the topic. So I return to my world, where I must provide solutions to concrete problems, make decisions that help myself and others to live.

Time goes by and everything seems to wilt.

In reality, we're the ones who no longer seek out the questions because we already know that only great faith in the existence of a word so often used and increasingly indefinable can buttress us. The word is Love.

Actually, I don't know what it means or represents. I do know its opposites well — hate and jealousy. I encounter them every day; I see them written in all the newspapers; I see them on TV.

What is Love? This is a question I continue to ask

myself even if it always comes back to me more cloaked in mystery and loaded with contrasting decisions to be made than before. However, it is a question that must be further explored without hoping for a convincing answer. It's a question that requires lengthy research and intuition.

These two different ways of coping with everyday reality make ours a relationship that is too draining.

~~~

Albert had begun seeing more of Greg again—and understanding him. At the time of his controversy with Joy, Greg had not been aware of the alienation that had been maturing within his spirit. Albert decided not to let him know that he had guessed what the problem was. Whenever they saw each other they spoke of the weather, business, friends—they were just killing a little time together, that's all.

This was good for Albert; it helped him to understand more about Joy, even if he felt like a spy trying to dig up information on his increasingly complicated relationship with her.

With the letter in the envelope, Albert felt liberated, though he immediately sensed a feeling of emptiness inside him, along with slight confusion and regret. He walked to the telephone to give Greg a call. They could spend a few hours together, do something pleasant. He picked up the receiver but had second thoughts. He hesitated. Suddenly he realized that he had no intentions of resuming that somewhat pathetic game of two adult men comparing accomplishments in order to feel gratified.

Albert already knew that the more he rummaged through his existence, the more excuses he found for not feeling gratified. He could not tell, however, whether it was to be blamed on other people or on the system as a whole. It was as though there was a plot afoot against his very desire to live, or worse, against his longing to live "simply."

He began thinking it out intensely — "Wasn't this the problem with the majority of humankind?" After Marianne's exit from his daily life, he became aware of a sensation of incompleteness within him which grew with the passing of the years. Each and every one of his attempts at avoiding such a state appeared, following a certain period of initial enthusiasm, to reach a point of non-interest.

Surely it was not all Joy's fault if he had misjudged how far the differences in their personalities would end up taking them. In the beginning he had also blown it with Marianne—but then unbeknownst, to him, a certainty had taken form. It appeared so unexpectedly real and concrete that in London it had driven him to say to her with conviction, "We're a couple. Actually we're *the* couple. Whether you like it or not."

~~~

His memory of that return trip to New York was still alive within him—the cab to the airport, the flight, and his excitement over the enormous surprise he experienced in reliving the moment in which he had been able to express to Marianne a concept that seemed so clear and obvious to him.

But how had it become so obvious that he could no longer explain it to himself? Towards the end of the flight, tired of all his why's, he had grown drowsy, but remained on edge, still amazed at what he had discovered about himself, and what he had succeeded in putting so simply into words.

Actually, that amazement had been brought down to size over the wear and tear of the years, with intensity that varied according to this or that period. It also led him to the conviction that those words uttered with such intensity many years before still represented his one and only certainty in life. What really sparked his curiosity was that this certainty was not born of reasoning, was not the fruit of philosophy or a sudden passion or even an overwhelming desire. It was certainty that had surfaced on his life's sea of nothingness which brought with it neither the promise of happiness nor sadness, neither good health nor tragedy, neither passion nor necessity. It was merely a reality that seemed to come from afar.

Where it had come from or where it was going was perhaps beyond his comprehension, at least during this hurried, fragile life.

At any rate, the way he interpreted his relationship with others had been forever swayed by this experience. Truly, he had to cut out all of this bustle, forget about trying to build new relationships, give up on achieving new professional or personal goals. From now on he would consider himself the only person who had actually come up with a certainty, albeit unexplainable. It did not matter whether or not one was aware that it might not be true, because he knew good and well that many others were in the same situation.

For Albert, Marianne lay at the center of all this, while for others the central focus may have been a god; another person, either real or imaginary; the sky; a creature of another species, such as a dog or a horse; one's country (in an abstract sense); one's homeland; a house; a tree; a mountain, etc.

Without realizing it, Albert was once again venturing into the secret history of humankind, reviewing the passions that have provided comfort to man during his painstaking progress amid the forces of nature, the forces of the universe, the forces of the soul, the forces of beliefs. Lots of theories, lots of suffering, lots of passions, lots of wars—all the result of not knowing how to utter a simple, nearly unexplainable word: Love.

Love that is born of nothing, just like Albert's very own words, and seems to vanish into nothingness.

~~~

Albert remained still and silent. He was at last content to live out the certainty he had found. "Love for a god or gods," he thought, "as in paganism so deplored today; love for a person, for one's country, for your house, your land, the stars, the sea, etc., is the single force that our lives are led by. It is a legitimate force which, however, must be cultivated in each of us, without negative interference from the outside world. Everyday life must go along its way, and we must live in that dimension whether we accept it or not. Love is ours, and it remains only for us and for those who share it with us. It requires no explanations, considerations, bonds or limits, because Love cannot distinguish them.

"Indeed, Love comes from nothing. If it is not accepted, it vanishes into nothingness. It is, however, a reality."

All this was too much for Albert. He had to go out and do something, get back into the daily routine even if it was Sunday, when anyone without anything else to do was free to do whatever he or she liked.

SUNSET IN SARASOTA

CHAPTER 26

Albert had enjoyed that catamaran outing not long ago. Since then he had found a place, not on the beach but in Sarasota Bay, that sold catamarans and he bought one. On this particular Sunday afternoon a fine wind was blowing, perfect for practicing his sailing skills.

It might have been more fun to go with Joy, but by himself he would be able to let his imagination run wild as his attentive gaze perused the sky, the clouds, the sea and the sails. Besides, he had already sent that letter to Joy.

Being alone would give him the chance to experience a virtual reality.

Indeed, now that he found himself out sailing in the bay, north of Ringling Bridge, in his mind he was able to overlap real images with ones that were products of his imagination so that the two seemed to meld.

He saw faces from his past life rush before his eyes. He relived situations that he believed forgotten—such as, for example, in that chalet in Vermont, when Jennifer asked him simply, "Why don't you ask Marianne to marry you?" Leaning up against the headboard of the bed, with those perfectly proportioned breasts of hers, she had inspired so much tenderness in him. In reality, at that moment the headboard was a large condo overlooking the bay, before which the catamaran was cutting. Jennifer herself was huge, sculpted in the light of Sarasota. He hadn't seen her after getting married to Marianne.

For Albert, Jennifer had become a precious memory to keep stored in the depths of his soul. Most likely she knew nothing of what had happened. Albert never called her—he didn't want to damage the expression on Jennifer's face which he kept within him. That night, or rather early morning, when she advised him to propose to Marianne, the expression she was wearing was that of a satisfied woman who tasted the pleasure of her own sacrifice by helping a mixed-up friend find his way.

Unfortunately, the events of September 11 had proven so terrible and hung in the air as if incomprehensible. In truth, Albert had always marveled at how New York, the center of the much envied capitalist world, had for so long remained immune to such heinous exhibitions of belligerence. There had been smaller attacks which could never match the kind of level that New York represented in the world.

America, seen from outside thanks to Hollywood and the mass media, seemed to be a country that was super-protected by a complex and efficient system. In actuality, its citizens enjoyed the free circulation of ideas, people and things without worrying too much about being too exposed to the evil of this world, envy. This is the true open character of America, and it must remain open even if forced to cope with further national tragedies.

If Albert had informed Jennifer about Marianne and 9-11, such an extremely concrete, live detail would have thrown her for a spiritual loop.

Before: She was the satisfied inspirational force thanks to whose good deed a happy ending was to unfold, at least in their imaginations—the union of Albert and Marianne. After: She would have felt like an instigator unaware of an event so loaded with drama and sadness for her friend Albert, even if she hardly knew Marianne at all. Surely the expression on her face would have changed and that beautiful memory of Jennifer that Albert carried within him would have been poisoned forever.

Call it egoism, call it self-defense, call it protecting another person's feelings. Call it whatever you want. But the fact was that Marianne had gone. Where, he did not know, and he did not care to talk about it with anyone. It was just a kind of awareness he had, whose details remained undefined. He did not wish to see sad faces over what had happened, or have people worried about his mental health.

Now he was out sailing, looking for something, though he knew not exactly what. His eyes darted from the clouds to the buildings, from the sails to the sea, from the sky to the city. He didn't want to admit it, but what he was really after was Marianne's face. He saw the faces of other friends he had known in his youth. He relived many of his life's details. He remembered meeting Marianne's parents before the wedding; he remembered them during the ceremony and after the news of 9-11.

But where was Marianne?

The only things that were certain—he had an office, a few building projects going on, a few good friends, and, if he wanted, he could dine with Joy that evening and make love with her, touching her still young and soft skin.

Was this all he could ask of life? How many people would have envied him? Yet he was confused and felt lonely. Everyone tried to offer suggestions and precise answers with regard to both work and his love life. He was still trying to think up the right questions. Marianne would have appreciated his mood.

Where was Marianne, anyway?

Sarasota, that beautiful little city kissed by good

fortune, glowed in the sun and warmth that began to fade as sunset approached. Was this paradise on earth now inspiring a claustrophobic reaction? He had to do something. He felt himself shake as if the eyes of the entire city were upon him.

He adjusted the sails and the catamaran picked up speed. He headed north, to catch the view of Sarasota Bay. Downtown Sarasota lay to the east and the sun to the west. He then turned back south. He sailed under the Ringling Bridge, with downtown still to the east, and Bird Key with its mansions, to the west. He continued in the same direction. The view changed. To the right was Lido Key Park, to the left the homes of Siesta Key. Further ahead lay semi-submersed sand dunes on the right, more houses on the left. Straight ahead was Big Pass—a highfaluting name for a pass betrayed by a superficial county administration whose lack of maintenance left it barely with a few feet of water.

At any rate, it was an imposing pass, with a grand stature that commanded respect—even if it should have been offended over the quantity of sand that suffocated it.

Indeed, sand was regularly pumped from the Gulf of Mexico onto the beaches, to the delight of swimmers and sunbathers. It never mattered much to the bureaucracy that the current, not having been informed of the new rules, wound up clogging this tenacious old pass.

The Big Pass was the Big Pass, an open invitation to the Gulf of Mexico.

The Gulf of Mexico—the mere utterance of that

name commanded respect. It is there that the currents are born which keep England and northern Europe warm and alive. The Gulf Stream is a great river, a great idea.

The catamaran made its way through the pass, leaving behind the dunes of sand to the right. Its double bow plowed through the waters, raising up sprays as it sailed over the light waves generated by a breeze coming from north-northwest.

Everything seemed perfect. As if it had been created all for Albert.

But where was Marianne?

He began to see his life pass before his eyes as if concentrated in a host of overlapped images in rapid succession. He revisited his most intense moments, as well as his dimmest. He was sailing briskly on the beam reach towards the setting sun. He had no idea why the boat was handling so well. Not being an expert sailor, he was unaware that this was the best point of sailing for a catamaran. He did know, however, that he had no particular destination in mind and was happy.

He flew across the waves as a way of returning to his origins, together with Marianne. He raced toward a safe place, be it for long or just briefly, to observe the world from outside. Perhaps time would no longer have any importance. We're not born wearing wristwatches.

He raced onward to become part of God, as time became a personal choice. The sun lay ahead and sunk into the sea, providing those unforgettable sensations to people up and down the beach. Who knows where they came from to see that nightly spectacle?

Land out ahead of his double bow was far off, too far off. He figured it would have been nearly impossible to reach it alone, with that tiny boat and without any provisions. Various descriptions of the currents of the Gulf of Mexico came to mind, as well as the so-called square waves.

He removed that thought, however, wondering what the future had in store for him.

He was day dreaming, there was absolutely no reason for him to be thinking. He recalled the theory of Hermann Hesse—he who thinks too much, drowns. Albert had no desire to drown just now, he was so enjoying being out on the ocean with the bright red sun lying straight ahead.

He spotted Marianne's face, as if projected upon the mainsail.

For an instant he turned his gaze and now Marianne's face appeared etched into the clear blue sky, which had been wiped free of clouds by the northern winds.

He saw himself running with arms open toward a beautiful woman with bright green eyes and long legs, who smiled at him as he was reaching her.

~~~

ABOUT
PIERO RIVOLTA

I literally grew up in a motor vehicle factory.

Day after day, from my earliest childhood, I lived amid the production lines of all sorts of two-, three- and four-wheel vehicles. The factory churned out quantities of motorcycles, mini-vans and, later, the famous Isetta—an egg-shaped city vehicle whose front door opened in such a way as to allow entry without ever having to bend down. We then moved to building sports cars (the various IsoRivolta models), snowmobiles, and a series of Formula 1 racers (the IsoRivolta Marlboro)—to name a few of our sexiest products.

The factory, our home and the extensive tree-covered grounds were all surrounded by the same wall, and life there was a kind of symbiosis of these three elements. The entire complex occupied most of downtown Bresso, a small town outside Milan, Italy. Inside that little world, successes and problems united people, animals and things.

Two well-defined classes of people gravitated round the facilities. There were those who were part of the factory organization, who either spent their days at the plant or worked beyond the gates to defend the firm's colors in other parts of Italy and abroad; and there were those from the outside world who came to us—customers, visitors and journalists. The former felt as if they belonged to one big family—a feeling that most of them retained even after moving on (myself included). The "outsiders," who often hailed from far and wide, were always thought of as friends of the business and the family and were treated accordingly.

With them, they brought a variety of customs, as well as problems that needed solving, and most of all, a boundless store of enthusiasm which, indeed, proved contagious. You see, at our factory we produced some very special, unique objects that men often fell in love with—perhaps because they had wheels and could be driven; perhaps because they went fast and never talked back.

My father had a magnetic personality and was extremely generous. He died in 1966 at the age of 57, during a slump in the business. I was 25 at the time, a newlywed with a degree in mechanical engineering that I'd received less than a year before from the Milan Polytechnic. I had to shift into high gear while still mourning the loss of my dad, whose passing left a scar in me that has never completely vanished.

Luckily, during my university years I had only attended those afternoon application sessions in which attendance was mandatory, while my mornings were spent at the plant. Even as a youngster, my favorite after-school activity had always been hanging round the factory. I still have warm memories of the friendships I made there. Though I never got the highest grades, I breezed through my engineering studies thanks to the rich human and practical experience I had gained inside my father's factory. Upon his passing I took the helm and was caught up by the same frenzy that had marked his life. I burned with the desire to create, take risks; I had inherited a credo of seeking out new experiences, knowledge, and sensations. Joy came in making new and beautiful things that procured happiness for us as well as for others. Most of all, my father had transmitted to me the longing to always be a free man, to be the master, as far as it is possible, of one's own destiny, able to assume life's responsibilities without being overly influenced by boards of directors, committees, religions and, especially, political ideologies and politics in general. His lifestyle had shown me that one could ignore geographical and cultural boundaries artificially set up by men, and look at the world with a much broader perspective. This vision of life, which he handed down to me, has led me along paths that at times have been quite difficult, paths where one is sometimes left standing powerless and looking on as positive human power is squandered and lost.

After experiences in different parts of Italy and the world, I literally dropped anchor—I arrived via sailboat—to the beautiful and cultured city of Sarasota, which lies on Florida's west coast, looking out across the Gulf of Mexico. It is here I hope to remain, until one day my ashes are dispersed by the waters of the Gulf.

I still keep that memory of the big yellow villa, my home in the green, wooded estate outside Milan, and of my life in that busy industrial city of northern Italy. My family still owns an apartment on the ground floor of the old villa, with a bit of yard just for ourselves, amid what has become Renzo Rivolta Park. I return every so often, when I can manage a break from my hectic schedule, and the place is like a safe, quiet oasis for me, where I am soothed by the house's thick walls, the trees I know one by one because I have watched them grow; some I even planted myself.

The need for open space and freedom inculcated in me by my father, along with his own strange physical need for adrenaline, have driven me to seek out a life brimming with experiences and changes. To begin with, I brushed aside all the rules which people usually adhere to if they want to make a successful career for themselves or simply become rich. The first of these rules is build yourself a resume, a business card that clearly identifies who you are, what you do and how you do it. You work to make this resume more and more credible until you reach a point where the system itself just drags you along. As long as you don't make any huge blunders, you've passed the test—you don't have to be first in the class any more, or prove that you yourself actually ever attained all that you set out to.

A publisher once asked me to write the story of my life. Who knows whether I'll ever have the time, or even whether it's been interesting enough to entertain readers? For now, I'd be stuck as to finding a fil rouge to make the whole thing comprehensible. All I can put on my business card is my name and the name of the company I work for, which are one and the same. There is one single constant in my life, though: the straightforwardness and stubbornness with which I cope with life's daily challenges.

On the work front, I've built sports cars, snow-mobiles and Formula 1 racers; I've raised horses in the country and managed a riding stable; I've de-signed and developed a variety of transport vehicles, including quadricycles, electric cars and buses. I've even organized music festivals, one of which I am particularly proud: La Musica, the International Chamber Music Festival in Sarasota. Over the years, I have constructed factories, directed a large textile mill; I have built office and apartment buildings, fairly large-sized communities, shopping centers, marinas; I have co-founded a bank. For many years I served as president of a prestigious golf club with a 36-hole course, one of my firm's projects (despite the fact that I don't actually play golf—I had to put up quite a front before various committees and at governors' meetings!). My latest madness involved the design and construction of yachts. I'm no longer a young fellow, but I still have plenty of projects in the hopper.

All of this surely runs against the grain when it comes to the cultural and economic trends of our times. Today, success is measured more in terms of quantity than quality. And it seems that only a pre-cise, repetitive and unrelenting marketing image can succeed in reaching sought-after sales results. This way of thinking doesn't bother me in the slightest, it's just that, unfortunately, I can't apply it—I can't live it. I consider this one of my limitations.

Sometimes I ask myself how I've been able to survive, keep my own company going (which, even though it is small, continues to enjoy excellent health) and to progress. I think that while quantity may mean business, passion and quality are protected by the spirit that makes the world go round. I look out and gaze upon the city lights in the distance, and listen to the far-off hum, entranced, indulging myself in the awareness of being a poet, in the same sense that we can all be poets.